A RAZOR'S EDGE

RICHARD WRIGHT

Copyright © 2021 Richard Wright

ISBN: 9798483054269

PublishNation
www.publishnation.co.uk

Acknowledgements

Thanks to my beautiful wife Elaine for her wisdom, prayers, and wonderful editing. To my children, Chris and Kate, for their support and their love. To my two wonderful tutors, Melanie Whipman and Claire Thurlow for their teaching, friendship, and insights, I am fortunate to have found you. To my dear friend, Professor Andrew Scott, who was always there with encouragement, for all my endeavours. To my honest first readers, Berwick, Mel, and Daniel, thank you for making this better. To the wonderful Baristas, Hazel & Marlena, at Café Nero, for serving excellent small, skinny cappuccinos and providing the perfect desk to write at. This novel is dedicated to the work of SAT-7.

ALL EVENTS TAKE PLACE IN 2019

CONTEST

There is a Prize of vinyl albums of your choice to the value of £70, or six-months music streaming cost. The winner is the person naming most of the following. The song lyric origin of the novel's title. The 21 album titles featuring the songs in the Chapter headings. Any album or song titles you can find in the story. When sending your answers please declare that Google or any other online searches were not used. Email me at rjwmarch@gmail.com before December 31st, 2021. Group entries are allowed but you have to share the prize.

This is a work of fiction. I have never been inside a police station in Cumbria, fired a sniper's weapon, sailed on Windermere, been on Morecambe sands, had a panic attack, attended an autopsy or been near a bombing. So apologies for any inaccuracies you may find, but they all suited the fiction and hopefully did not spoil the enjoyment of the story.

Part One

Guilt

There is a way that seems right to a man, but its end is the way of death.

Proverbs 14:12

1

Something in the night

July 15th

The silver Audi hatchback slid to a silent halt, the sole occupant of the car park below Wray Castle. Dressed all in black, the driver unlocked the boot and took out the single canvas bag. It was a short walk down the path into the woods. Ten minutes later, walking past a dilapidated boathouse, the four stumps in the gravel path came into view, marking the turn to Lake Windermere's shore, to the perfect spot assessed the day before. A foot high, the rocky outgrowth from the bracken was perfect for his special weapon. He set the alarm for 6:45 AM, laid down on the bracken and fell asleep.

Kim Givens raised the Wayfarer's sail, heading out to the centre of the lake. At her height and build, she could manage a Wayfarer but nothing much larger. Windermere was her daily lake of tranquillity before the drive over Wrynose and Hardknott passes to her work at Sellafield.

If the winds were up, the Wayfarer bounced over the dark depths, or, on a still sunny day like today, she just glided. She looked out for Wray Castle a mile away on the far shore to keep her bearings. In the middle of the Lake, she stood, holding the mast, the light breeze blowing her blonde locks across her eyes. She took a band from the pocket of her shorts, to make a ponytail. At 7:00 AM she was alone out on the lake. She held onto the mast and peered into the grey unknown of the deep lake. She never heard the whistling sound approaching her head.

DCI Diana Petrou sat bolt upright in bed, soaked in sweat from the same recurring nightmare ever since February 23rd. She was lying on the ground, thrown over by a flying grey cloud, tearing through her clothes, shaving away a layer of skin. Her eyes opened to an atrium of carnage and a rising crescendo of desperate screams and wailing. The death cloud settled onto a floor of bloody, torn bodies. Eight were motionless, others crying for loved ones, but Affredi's body was a mere memory, plastered to the walls.

Awake, instead of tears all she felt was bloody rage at her own guilt and shame. Seeing that one moment when Affredi's thumb hovered over that red button.

She carried her cappuccino and buttered toast out on to the apartment balcony. She fidgeted in her wicker chair and pulled down her T Shirt. She stirred the froth, stretched out her legs and placed her feet up on the railings.

Two months recuperating from the bombing, in the Lake District, the after-effects remained unchanged, though being with the Windermere police was easier. The triple fault of being half Greek, an avowed Christian, and a woman, separated her from most of the city colleagues she left behind. She always suffered some familiar abuse and refused to attend the clubs and gatherings her male colleagues indulged, proud of her reputation for not bending the rules to get a conviction.

The city pace was furious, with murders, burglaries, gang fights and frauds. Here in the Lakes, the pace was sedate, only called for a petty theft or a closing time brawl. Being given an apartment with an aspect over Lake Windermere into the morning sunrise was a bonus. She took another bite of toast and thought nothing serious ever happened here.

Looking out over Lake Windermere Diana could see a single dinghy. It seemed insignificant against the backdrop of the fells. The lone sailor took down the sail. From this distance she was convinced it was a woman. She was standing, holding on to the mast, peering into the lake. Diana's concentration was broken by a ringtone.

'Morning Ma'am'

It was her DC, Stephanie Giles. To Diana she was too sarcastic, resented this DCI foisted on her.

'The boss has asked for us pronto.'

'I'm finishing breakfast, what's the matter?'

'A baby abandoned in the grounds of the General.'

'I'm not missing my morning run; see you in an hour.'

Diana put down the phone determined to finish her coffee. Her attention turned back to the Lake. The boat seemed empty. She reached back for her phone.

'Giles, do me a favour, send someone out on the lake right now, to check a dinghy. Only one out on the lake, maybe half a mile from my place. It did have a woman on board but not anymore. Get it checked in case she's gone overboard.'

'Will do.'

2

What's goin' on?

July 15th

Diana stood in front of Superintendent Julian Ingles. Diana knew his type. At fifty-six, hoping for a trouble-free ride to retirement and displaying a misogyny she hadn't experienced for the last few years. His spreading physique showed his years behind a desk and having golf as his sole recreation. She already knew Ingles didn't like her and didn't trust her and Diana felt the same way. She stared at the mournful face under a receding grey hairline.

Ingles started. 'We have an abandoned baby. First priority Di.'

'That's Diana.'

'Pardon?'

'My name is Diana, not Di, given to me by my mother. So it's either Diana or my rank. I don't like to be diminished.'

'Apologies, DCI Petrou. As I was saying, the first priority is to find the mother. You and Giles to go to the hospital and quiz the staff. All the usual, any witnesses, CCTV, get forensics on the blanket and the baby's clothes.' Diana turned to go. 'Giles tells me you sent someone to check a boat on the lake.'

'Maybe nothing.'

It was a twenty-minute journey to the Royal Hospital. DC Stephanie Giles, sat in silence in the passenger seat, until her phone rang. 'Ma'am, that call was about your boat, it was empty. They found a cardigan and a security badge for Sellafield with the name Kim Givens.'

Diana hated suicides. She knew she should feel pity but her compassion was for those left behind. 'Tell me about the baby.'

'Girl, two days old, outside the Royal, wrapped in a blanket, no distinguishing marks. We did find other stray hairs on the blanket.'

'Giles, see if the boat has any hairs and get a DNA match done. I don't believe in coincidences.'

They drew a blank at the hospital, no-one saw the baby being left but there was CCTV to go through. Back in Windermere Diana strolled into the grimy squad room. Nothing more than four walls in urgent need of a coat of paint with a random collection of desks and chairs along with an ageing white board. The walls bore the marks of torn Sellotape and Blutac remnants. Sergeant Collins barred Diana's way, waiting to hand her a file.

'Ma'am, we've just got a report in. A body was washed up on Windermere's shore near Brockhole. It was a young woman. We've requested a DNA match to the missing baby and an autopsy for the body.'

'So,' Diana sighed, 'a suicide,' and walked away.

Collins shouted after her. 'Ma'am, it's not suicide, she was shot.'

Diana swung around. 'What? I saw that dinghy, she was alone.'

'Ma'am, there's a PC on the scene, he says she was shot through the head.'

Diana should have felt ashamed for her sudden moment of excitement; a real case was about to start. Diana beckoned Giles into her office. 'I never saw anyone else out on the lake. So she was shot from a distance, and in the head not the body. Giles that's at least five hundred yards and is a hell of a shot. We have a murder, and this is no ordinary murder. What the hell was this girl mixed up in?

'I'll see about her movements the day before, Ma'am.'

'Giles, Ma'am makes me feel about eighty.'

'What do we call you Ma'am?'

'You and you alone can call me Di. Now, back to Givens, delve into her personal life, relatives, boyfriends, whatever she was employed as at Sellafield. I'm going to examine the boat again. Call me when they've identified the bullet calibre.'

Diana called to Giles as she turned to go. 'How about a drink after we finish.'

'I'm playing football tonight; tomorrow would be OK. And you can call me Steph.'

She spun on her trainers and left.

3

Wake up.

July 16th

One month here, Diana still wasn't used such peaceful mornings, or the clean smell in the air. All different to waking at home. The shouts at the bairns to get out of bed, the spaniels barking at any intrusive noise, the constant drone of the traffic of life speeding up the ring road, into the city centre. She preferred that smell of dust and tarmac. She was a city woman born and bred and missed James, missed the kids. Five months on from the bombing, little had changed, she was damaged and vulnerable. There were four more sessions of therapy to go through. Fool the therapist and she would be signed off and then go home.

It could be a good time to go back to Santorini, to see her mother on the anniversary of the bastard's death. It amazed her how her Mum thought her Dad was the perfect man. She inherited little from her Dad, thankfully, but from her Mum, her determination, and grey, blue eyes.

Leaving the apartment, her clothes looked like she slept the night in them, which, in her case, was true. Her favourite creased, thin, black crew neck under her familiar black trouser suit. The same every day. The last ten years she dispensed with a handbag, always left behind when chasing some miscreant, in favour of a backpack. Its contents were a smartphone, whistle, deodorant, pens, spare hair bands, hairbrush, notebook, flash stick, and a compact. She wore little make-up and never lipstick or eyeliner. Walking down the road, she tied back her shoulder length, dark hair into a bun and put on her old Ray-Bans. A few minutes' walk from the apartment, Diana sauntered into the nearest coffee shop.

Her favourite barista greeted her with a welcoming smile. Twenty years of age, her brown locks tucked under a baseball cap.

'Usual Diana?'

Hazel repeated herself before Diana took notice.

'Oh, yes, the usual.'

'Small skinny cappuccino, chocolate on top, with an extra shot, coming up.'

'Today, two extra shots.'

'Rough night?'

'Rough life.'

She nodded to the familiar customers, reading the Daily Mail, wishing for a world they recognised.

'Here you go Diana, hope it'll be a good day.'

'Fat chance. See you soon.'

The remote opened the garage door to her singular indulgence, a top of the range VW Tiguan SUV. Settled in the leather seat, she connected her iPhone on Bluetooth and thought about what music suited the pleasant ride down into Windermere. Bruce of course, The Boss and his song, 'Thunder Road'. She sang along with the first words, changing the heroine's name to her own, forcing it to scan. 'Diana's dress waves.'

The A591 was trouble free till reaching the centre of Windermere. The summertime grockles were already tumbling out into the road, bringing traffic to a halt. She'd already learnt these were the people who never got further than a tea shop or Dove Cottage or the Lake's edge. Always admiring the scenery from afar but never getting amongst it. She might be a city type, but she knew the fells from coming here several times with the family. She learnt that walking the fells was where you appreciated its beauty and danger too. The fells were like life. A known path lost and you were on the way to disaster. You needed a guide to show you the right way.

Twenty minutes later, striding, into the nick, Giles stood up from her desk. 'The Super's asking for you.'

Ingles didn't gaze up from his desk. He ushered Diana into his office with a cursory flick of his fingers. 'I'm told the woman from the dinghy was murdered, and we have identified her. What's the plan?'

'It's early days yet, all the usual.'

Diana sensed the impatience listening to Ingles prattle. 'Clues, theories?'

Diana couldn't resist a dose of sarcasm. 'Oh, if it's theories, could be a jealous partner, could be a random psycho with a gun, all sorts of possibilities.'

'You think this is bloody funny? You are supposed to be the detective. Pull your finger out. Get me answers. Dismissed!'

She slammed the door, thinking, 'Idiot, all bark and no bite, save us from provincial cops.'

Later that day, a woman came into Windermere Police Station with a picture of her missing daughter, Kim Givens. It matched the body washed up. Diana tried her hardest for a sympathetic tone.

'Can you describe Kim?'

'Kim was a lovely daughter, with a sweet round face and gentle eyes. When she spoke it was never shrill. She was smart but not always with people. She grew up without being sceptical, assumed others meant the best. I worried about her of late, she was involved with a drug dealer in Keswick, but she wasn't pregnant.'

'Who was the dealer?'

'Dan Jetty.'

Diana thought, was it possible Jetty possessed the skill to shoot, to kill a victim from half a mile? That would take a trained professional.

'Mrs Givens, we will interview you again but I apologise, our priority is to identify the body. Detective Giles will take you.

Again, I am sorry for your loss and be assured, we will find her killer.'

Giles waited for Mrs Givens to leave the office. 'Jetty's well-known to us. Always a suspect but we've never had enough proof to charge him, no witnesses willing to go on the record. He's like a weed coming up through the concrete, surviving against the odds but still a weed.

'OK. Can you take her to the morgue?'

At the end of the day, Diana bellowed through the glass for Giles. Always dressed the same way, blue, tight jeans, white trainers, and T Shirts pronouncing her favourite bands. Today's choice was a classic, The Ramones. 'Steph, what did we get from the drug dealer Jetty, about him and about the girl?'

Giles planted herself in the one spare chair. 'We haven't tracked him down, appears to have gone to ground. We have a DNA test coming on the woman and baby to see if they match.'

'Clues on Jetty, what do we know about him?'

Giles rolled out a familiar tale. 'He's been arrested a lot of times after arriving here as a twelve-year-old from Belfast. He started with petty theft, was expelled from school, graduated onto running dealers in Ambleside, Keswick, Barrow, and up to Carlisle. Kim was his girlfriend for six months, but other informants reckoned she dumped him. The sole sighting on the night of the fifteenth was Jetty in the Wansfell Arms, drinking with a woman who the bartender reckoned was Givens.'

Diana wondered what she was doing. No reason to kill her or have her killed. She didn't think Jetty could make that shot either, but worth keeping an eye on him, to get him for dealing, if nothing else.

Diana rested her chin on her clasped hands with her eyes closed. After a minute Giles broke the silence.

'Owt else Di?'

'Where did she work?'

'Like her mother said, at Sellafield. She was the personal assistant for one of the senior managers, Mark French.'

'Has anyone spoken to him?'

'No, not yet.'

'Well, you handle that. Get Martins to check on her associates, any former boyfriends?'

Giles smiled straight at Diana with a sly smirk, 'Thanks, wouldn't have thought of that.'

'Before that, where do we find this Jetty character.'

'Last we knew he was living with his mother still.'

Diana stared. 'Ok, we'll go to her and when we get back, go to Sellafield. Tonight, you and Martins do an all-night surveillance on his known haunts. If you see him, keep me informed where he goes, who he talks to, what he does, if you can manage that.'

The smirk returned across Giles's lips. 'Of course. I'll call you every hour with an update.'

4

Rip this joint.

July 17th

Killing without leaving a clue takes preparation and patience and the right armament for the task. His weapon of choice was an Accuracy International AWM with a folding wooden stock. It was the sniper's choice in Afghanistan and Iraq, with a range of 1604 metres and muzzle velocity of 936 meters per second. The sniper used the larger maximum length cartridges and a five round, detachable magazine block. Every element of the rifle, was taken apart, cleaned, re-assembled fastidiously before being used and it fitted perfectly into a bulky leather holdall. Handling the rifle, it was like a surgeon holds a scalpel, or a painter a brush.

The sniper lay perfectly still on the bracken by Lake Windermere. The rifle was rested on the same rocky outgrowth, as two days before, waiting for the target, in the cross hairs of the telescopic sight. Twenty minutes passed before the silver yacht came into view, sailing slowly towards the fate of the man standing at the wheel. There was no rain and only a slight easterly wind to compensate for. His finger and thumb made miniscule changes to the sight.

A forefinger wrapped around the trigger, and the sniper felt, no emotion, no recognition it was a human being about to die, just an object to prove a perfected skill. The head of Adam Wilson entered the crosshairs, the trigger squeezed, and the bullet flew. One second later it smashed through the left ear, tearing apart the cortex. The man fell backwards, over the side and into the water. A second bullet, unrequired, was shot into the depths of the lake. The suppressor, at this distance couldn't stop

13

the sonic crack but disguised its direction for any unsuspecting audience.

The rifle was disassembled into the bag. Walking backwards, a brush swept away any footprints till he reached the gravel path. The assassin swung the bag over his shoulder, zipped up his jacket and walked on, only feeling elated satisfaction, an urge satiated.

Diana peered at the panel of name plates. 'Here we are, Carol Jetty.'

It took several rings on the intercom before a woman answered. 'Is that Mrs Jetty, I'm DCI Petrou, with my colleague DC Giles. Can we come in? We need to talk to your son.'

'What's he done this time? He hasn't lived here for ten months, got his own digs in Ambleside.

'We would still like a few words.'

'OK, come in if you must. I'm on the second floor.'

The rooms and Mrs Jetty were both a surprise. Both were elegant, tasteful. Mrs Jetty was late forties, shoulder length loose, styled blonde locks on a slim figure. The vermillion red lipstick seemed too garish in contrast. They took the offered seats. She launched into a speech about knowing her son's record, how he's mixed up in drugs, always in dubious company, which is why she threw him out. The condemnation was laid on the father, who abandoned them years ago. Giles inquired about her son's whereabouts. The reply was curt. If he showed at her door, she wouldn't let him in, or answer the phone to him. Diana thought, what was it about her demeanour that suggested she was lying?

She decided to alter tack, 'Have you come across Kim Givens?'

'Yes, why?'

'She was found dead yesterday in Lake Windermere, murdered.'

She remarked, that's awful, but her sentiment seemed hollow. She claimed Kim was a sensible girl, who couldn't stand Dan's entourage and didn't take drugs.

'I told her, he's a crook, always will be. Detective, I can't believe he has anything to do with this. He's a dealer, a thug, not a murderer.'

Giles broke in. 'How would Dan handle rejection?'

'Same as all the other girlfriends. The person Dan cares about most is himself. Kim did say she was suffering some problems at Sellafield and was considering leaving. It was about her boss. Kim was an intuitive sort, good with people, always believed others meant the best.'

Giles pressed on. 'What else you can tell us, like where your son was on the morning of the 15th?'

'No. I told you I scarcely see him.'

As Diana stood up, she offered over her business card, staring into Carol's eyes, thinking, what is she hiding. 'If you remember anything else or if Dan gets in touch, call me on this number. We'll let ourselves out.'

Outside, Diana offered Giles a polo mint. 'Steph, what do you think, you buy all that?'

'No. Seemed phoney. She was lying.'

Diana nodded in agreement. 'Get her phone records checked, ask around, see if it's true that they don't see one another. Could she be involved in his business?'

Giles asked. 'Did Givens have a secret about Jetty, about a deal going down, maybe threatened him?'

'Maybe. Let's both go exploring before the press conference this afternoon.

Diana's phone rang, it was DC Martins

'Ma'am, they've found another body. It's on the far side of Windermere, a body washed up on the shore. A man, late 40s they reckon.'

'Text me the location. Is the pathologist on his way?'

'Yup, Blackpool's already arrived.'

15

'Who?'

'Blackpool, Richard Sands.'

'Local humour, pathetic.'

Thirty minutes later Diana and Giles, in wellies and protective garb, were standing by the shore, attending the pathologist performing his rituals. Getting impatient, Diana barked. 'Can you clean off his head, and lift his hair up?'

Blackpool stood up, hands on his hips, annoyed. 'Why?'

'Humour me.'

Blackpool lifted the wet hair.

'Shit, shot through the top of the head. Blackpool we will need pictures. How long has he been in the water?

'Only a few hours; I'll tell you more when I autopsy, and if it's the same bullet we found in the Givens woman. No identification on him, but maybe a clue in an abandoned yacht.'

Giles interrupted. 'Di, I know him, that's Adam Wilson, I went to school with his son Mel. He owns a local construction firm. Any major project locally, he's usually involved.'

'Steph, we need to see if there's any connection with Givens, any reason to kill them both, otherwise there's the good news, we've got a serial killer, a psycho and an expert sniper.'

5

Speak to me.

July 18th

Cold sweats followed the shaking. Diana steadied herself against the back wall to hold on for fear of fainting. Her head was full of broken ice. She took repeated breaths, to slow her heart rate. Ingles was already halfway through a prepared statement, summarising the two murders, before he called on Diana to give an update and how the press could help. She blinked at the sudden illumination of electronic flashes, and muttered to herself, 'Time to get a grip.'

She'd given press conferences a hundred times before but couldn't shake the thought of breaking down in front of all these journalists. The method of the murders attracted the national and Cumbrian newspapers. She mumbled a few words before walking straight out of the room.

Giles grabbed her arm. 'You, OK?'

'I forgot my notes, tell them I'll be back,'

Back in her office, she shut the blinds, locked the door, laying prostrate on the floor, swallowing two pills. All she could do was wait until the panic subsided. The medication was for the pain of the scars. It helped with the panic too. It was a few minutes later that Giles rattled the door.

'The door's locked. Ingles says get back, otherwise the press will leave.'

Diana stood up and unlocked the door. 'I was feeling nauseous, needed to take a moment. Let's go.'

Walking up to the mikes, she held her right hand aloft. 'Ladies and gentlemen, apologies, I forgot some notes. Superintendent

Ingles has told you the identity of the deceased and the method of these murders. The one connection we can establish this far is the way they have been killed. We are further investigating their movements over the last four days and their known associates to see if we can identify a motive. Will now take questions.'

The first question was not unexpected.

'John Easter, Daily Mirror. Detective, this is what we have been told; two people have been shot from a distance who appear unconnected. Are we dealing with a serial killer?'

'I think it's wrong to suggest that before our investigation has begun.'

'Excuse me, you're saying that the investigation hasn't started yet?'

Diana gripped the podium tight. 'The murders have happened in the last few days. We are at first stages; just received the initial post-mortem results, which we shared with you today.'

The journalist waved his notebook. 'You are saying that this is not a random killing.'

'No, I am saying that we are at early stages, to speculate on random killing is irresponsible journalism, it would cause local panic.'

A collective gasp rang from the assembled journalists.

'Did you call us irresponsible? We can quote you on that.'

Before Diana could say another word, Ingles stood up. 'Ladies and gentlemen, let me explain. We have several possible motives in cases like these. What DCI Petrou is trying to say is that at this stage assuming one cause won't help us getting to the truth. We are, of course, not suggesting irresponsibility. DCI Petrou will apologise for any such inference.'

Ingles pleaded that any information stuck to the facts laid out and to request the public's help if they have seen Miss Givens or Mr Wilson in the days before their murders.

'The families have of course been informed. They are in conversation with the Police and let's leave them to their grieving.'

Diana left, Giles and Martins trailed behind in silence until they returned to the Police Station, confronted by Ingles.

'What the hell was that! These people are vital to the investigation. The press tomorrow isn't going to be the murders it's going to be you, questioning your capability to be in charge of this. That was a total screw up. Why did you disappear at the beginning? Eh? Don't bother answering, I'll talk to you later when I've calmed down, to make a decision about your future.'

Martins whispered to Giles, 'What's going on, what's wrong with her?'

An hour later Diana caught up with Giles leaving the building.

'Steph thank you for today. I have to apologise to you for how I've been. You are a fine copper. You're intelligent, savvy, committed but I can see I made a few wrong judgements. I did arrive with an attitude of the city, resented being sent here.'

'Thank you for that. I think we resented you being here too.'

Diana turned smiling. 'We must work together, be a partnership. Ingles is a promoted idiot. Between us we have the experience to crack this. So, let's start over.'

Giles offered a handshake with a grunt of approval.

'Hi, I'm Steph pleased to meet you. Can I get you a drink?'

They sat in a corner of the lounge of The Wansfell Arms, where the décor and the patrons both had seen better days, cradling two pints of Theakstons. Steph broke the silence. 'Tell me what happened. If we are going to be partners on this, let me in on what happened to you, I won't share it.'

Diana stared at Steph, wondering if she could trust her. The woman with the neat black hair, large dark brown eyes and the most disarming of smiles, like a young Sade.

Diana was taping her feet on the stone floor. 'OK. It's a hangover from the bombing. When it went off, I managed to turn and drop to the floor in time. When I stood again it was carnage. All I could see were bits of people on a blood smattered floor. Anyone alive was screaming and coughing from the grey, thick cloud, I was cut to pieces too.'

Diana's head dropped as she spoke, her hand instinctively covering her mouth.

'Di, you don't have to go on.'

'It's OK, you should know all this. I ignored all the warnings and went straight back to work. The first homicide I went to I suffered a panic attack. It was a jumper and we needed to work out if he committed suicide or was pushed. The evidence of the body, its position, its injuries can help you distinguish. This one was splayed out, face down blood pouring from his head and torso, it only took one look and the panic started, sweats, shaking but inside was worse. How do you describe fear, its darkness, desolation? I ran away and collapsed into a shop doorway wondering if this would end. I put my head between my legs and cried out, save me. Since, I have nightmares and get up hoping each day will be better. What's that saying? Hope springs eternal, not for me.'

'I didn't realise, you've kept it well hid.'

Diana looked up with a half-smile. 'It's more like one of those geysers that explodes unexpectedly, then disappears. Anyroad, I agreed to go for two months therapy and take some medication. They suggested one way to ease me back in was to take the opportunity to transfer here and I've walked straight into this. I am better than I was; the medication is helping. Today it was the sudden barrage of lights that triggered the panic. There's this too.'

Diana rolled up her sleeve. The whole arm was scared, lined, discoloured. Steph went to touch it, Diana flinched back. 'Sorry, that's instinctive. My right side's the same. Over time it will fully heal.'

'Wow. That's why on a hot day you always wear something long sleeved. Di, what can I say? I promise you; I won't share this with anyone. I'm here for you.'

'Thank you, why don't you tell me about you.'

'Not a lot to say. I'm a real local, hence the soft, delightful accent. I'm twenty-nine, single, live with flatmate Martine in

Ambleside, where I grew up. My Dad's business was providing rowing boats on Windermere, he's retired. My Mum was always the housewife bringing up me and my older brother. She came here from Antigua, waitressing in an Ambleside hotel. Met my Dad and theirs was a proverbial marriage made in heaven.'

'And joining the force?'

'It was a presentation at school about careers in the Police, that's what inspired me to join up after I finished Uni. With my computing degree I was put on all sorts of IT tasks at first. But watching others performing, I got the ambition to be a detective. Sat the exams and here I am. I know you have a husband and kids what about your wider family?'

'Dad, Nikos, was Greek, met my Mother who was working as a tourist rep. When she finished that job, we came back to the UK. He died a year ago from cancer. You've seen that thing when you knock over a glass of wine on a table. You try to stop it spreading; inevitable it evades you, dripping onto the floor. His cancer was like that. He wasn't a pleasant man. My Mother's still alive and went back to Santorini after he died, to be with the rest of the family.'

'Di, I'm confused, you're married but your surname sounds Greek. Petrou.'

'That's my maiden name. I was single when I joined the force and decided not to change when I got married. That's enough reminiscing.'

Steph smiled at Diana and changed the subject. 'Have we got a serial killer? What's the profile?'

'In this case. He's an expert shot. He kills from a distance, feels cold, detached, sees the people as objects. Gets his thrill from the skill of the shot. It's the act of killing, not the demise itself. That shows in choosing random targets. Maybe he got satisfaction before from legitimate killing.

'Ahh, an Army man, a sniper.'

'What about gun clubs?

21

'A couple of nearby ones, but he could have come from anywhere; we have tourists all year round. The best option is the Army.

'But of course, he might not be British. I say again, the incidence of serial killers in the UK is rare and we haven't had an incident where people are killed like this. In America they have rooftop killers choosing random targets, fanatics in Churches mass murdering, incidents like Columbine or Las Vegas, but not quite like this. Here we have a single, skilled killing and on another day the same killing in the same locale and same manner. If he is a serial killer, he's saying, you can't find me. Unless we find the site where he shot from, the sole forensics is the bullet. I bet they turn up clean too.'

'Is it a man?'

'Unless you can find a record of a trained female sniper, it's almost certainly a man. I am worried that Ingles gets us chasing down the path of it only being a serial killer route, when to me it's possible we have a person who has killed these two people deliberately. Let's see if they have any connection.'

'What do we do in the meantime, with the press, with the public?'

'A dilemma again. If we tell the public what we may have, the result could be panic. People will stop using the lake. What would our sniper do? Choose, I bet, to kill somewhere else, say up in the fells. We say nothing, except, pursuing our enquiries. Sad to say, we may know a lot more if he kills again. You, me, Martins let's chase down any connections between Kim Givens and Adam Wilson. Did Wilson have business with Jetty or at Sellafield, or were they connected on the drugs business? Draw up a list of people to interview, Givens colleagues at Sellafield, Wilson's son, his employees. Tell Ingles we will pursue the serial killer line. I'll carry on too with this death on Blencathra, that's a Sellafield link too. Did we get nothing at all from the all-nighter you did on Jetty?'

'Thanks again for that. No, he didn't show. We did spot one person familiar to us, Cody Beck; we should interview her.'

6

I know there's an answer.

July 19th

Julian Ingles convened his detective team into a makeshift incident room in Windermere station. With him was Petrou, Giles, DC Harry Martins, his station Sergeant, Fiona Collins and two PCs. Diana's arrival brought the necessary experience, in a place where murders were few and far between. Diana suggested calling in favours from her own nick.

Ingles attempted being diplomatic. 'Diana, I will let you know if we need extra resources, but the challenge always is budget. Let's make a start with what we've got. OK, let's begin with Kim Givens, Martins you can scrawl.'

Giles read aloud her notes on the interview with Givens Mother.

'Kim was twenty-four, according to the mother a sensible girl, until the last few months. Got 'A' Levels and a job at Sellafield. as P.A. to one of the bigwigs, the COO, Mark French. She argued with the mother about her boyfriend Daniel Jetty who we have inside knowledge is a drug dealer. The mother insists Kim never took drugs.'

Diana noticed that Ingles seemed to react at the name Mark French. Ingles offered. 'I have met Mr French once; he was with other people at the nineteenth hole after a round of golf.'

Diana thought, you bloody liar. Ingles kept talking. 'We first thought suicide without knowing the reason. The findings are she was shot. A killing out of the ordinary. Shot from half a mile away, who can make that shot?'

The room was silent.

'That was a question for anyone to chip in.'

24

Martins thought he'd offer an opinion. 'Well the lakes is full of people with guns, like the farmers.'

Ingles retorted. 'Think before you speak. They have shotguns, not long-range weapons. The bullet was clean, no trace of fingerprints. The wound suggests an aerodynamic with hollow point, which colleagues, suggests what?'

Giles wagged her finger at him. 'Super, quit the patronising. It suggests a sniper shot. Having a gander at Gun Club members or maybe ex-Army.'

Ingles pointed at her. 'Alright you two. Martins, get a record of the Gun clubs in the area and lists of their members to check against the PNC. Giles, liaise with the Army through MOD. Request a list of ex-army for last twenty years of trained snipers.'

Diana laid out the interview with Jetty's mother. He didn't live with her anymore or been seen at his flat in Ambleside, she'd put out an APB. She appeared to be content he is out of her life. She spoke to Kim Givens, though was loathed to admit it at first. She explained Kim was having problems with her boss, nothing more. She promised to tell us if Jetty was in contact, not that Diana believed her, from her body language and utterances.

Ingles glanced at Giles who nodded agreement. 'Why was she on the Lake?'

Diana answered. 'A regular sailor since she was twelve. It was her dinghy. She went out most mornings before heading off.'

Ingles perked up. 'A routine anyone could find out. Ok, let's go through the second murder. Diana?'

'Adam Wilson, fifty-four, owner of his own construction firm. Son Mel and daughter Isabel, who both work for the firm. From reputation and lack of competition his company is involved in most of the area's major contracts. Is he prominent on the Rotary, Chamber of Commerce, friendly with local councillors and plays golf?'

Ingles smirked. 'Thanks for the insinuation Diana. I met him at the golf course. I can't comment on his friendships. Nothing in the past has suggested any corruption on contracts, not with the rules in situ over tenders. He's been in business here for years. What else?'

Giles jumped in. 'Well he was a regular sailor on Windermere too and guess what, he sailed from the same marina, Low Wood. Blackpool confirms he was shot in a similar way to Givens. I'm thinking he was shot from the same spot on the far shore. Again. no fingerprints on the bullet. A single shot, we guess, from a considerable distance on the lake shore. We found nothing on his boat.'

Ingles asked. 'Nothing at all?'

Steph nodded. 'Nope, it was like it was stripped bare, having it checked for fingerprints.'

'A killer who shoots from a distance but goes back to the scene of the crime. Doesn't sound sensible to me. Who else might do that? What was he hiding on the boat?'

Steph broke the silence.

'What theories do we have for these two murders committed in the same way.'

Diana held her hand to stop Steph talking. 'It's too early to say. Is it tied in with Jetty and drugs? One is a young woman at Sellafield, the other has no contact with her, could speculate, that given their ages Wilson's kids might recognize her from school. Of course, the worst scenario, we have a nutter with a gun picking off random targets. A man with a compassion bypass. How likely is a serial killer? Nothing yet to discount it. I hate to say it but we may only know that if another similar murder happens. It's a skilled killer with superior skills and special equipment.

Ingles stood. 'Let's dig deeper. Priority is to find Jetty. Collins, take the PCs, do a tour of the pubs in Ambleside, Keswick, and Windermere tonight. Martins when you get a list of gun clubs in the county, inquire if they have anyone who has been trouble or was kicked out. Another possibility is the military, but that could be someone from another country. Giles let's start with our forces. Make enquiries for those trained snipers. Giles, go see Wilson's kids. Go easy, see if they know any connection at all to Givens. Diana, go over to Sellafield. Interview this Mark French, see if he has any connection to Wilson.'

7

Let down.

July 20th

The louder Catherine shouted his name, the faster he ran. Berwick Stewart only stopped when her voice evaporated into the wind. Vivid visions flashed of her and Mark entwined. He picked up a misshapen stone, trying to squeeze the pain away, forcing his palm scarlet red. He hurled it high before hollering, 'You Bastards!'

He didn't deserve this. She cheated with of all people his boss, Mark French. Desolate tears flowed, thinking of the months of lies, of phony friendship. How could he go to Sellafield tomorrow, to talk to him? Could he ever forgive her?

The darkening clouds made him take his bearings. Red kites were circling above, harbingers of threatening weather and the urgency to get off the fell. The way to avoid her was to go back the way they came. That meant going down Sharp Edge. Near the summit of Blencathra, Sharp Edge emerges. An aptly named arete between rocky crags, a climb for those with nerves of steel over its razor-sharp crests.

Five minutes later Berwick was standing on a threshold, feeling anguish in his stomach. The blue sky was replaced by a clinging shroud of mist coming in and the once dry path was doused. From above he could make out the craggy outcrops but the sheer drops either side were fading in the mist. The first challenge was the steep scree of Foule Crag to reach the Edge itself. What started as hazardous became precarious. Good sense told him to descend facing the rockface. His legs were shaking from fear, realising any wrong step could be fateful. Before he reached the Edge, one loose rock pulled his foot sideways. His body began to slide downwards. The scree tore into his bare arms, his hands grasped for a hold. It was his foot hitting a larger boulder that brought him to a halt. He lay motionless, his heart beating, blood seeping from his forearms.

A voice called out of the mist. 'You, OK?'

The voice was followed by a dark shape in shadow behind torch light, offering a helping hand.

'Bloody hell, your arms are a mess. I saw you slide. Was too far away to get to you. Can I help?'

'I must watch out where I'm putting my feet. I've walked up Sharp Edge lots of times, but never down.'

The walker stepped forward, laying down a backpack. 'Let me help you if you are on your own.'

Berwick peered behind. 'Yup, just me. I'll get on though, I'm already late. I can deal with this, you carry on.'

'If you're sure. The mist is closing in, why don't you walk on with me, might be safer.'

'No, I'll be fine. Thanks all the same.'

Berwick strode past, shrieking as a small ice pick struck the back of his head, dead centre. Lent on, the point gauged a bigger hole, easing on through the giving flesh, the crunching sound of the cranium splitting and into the soft cortex, tearing it apart. Berwick fell, his body twitching, blood oozing from the corners of his mouth. The walker, picked him up, twisted him around and peered down into his eyes. Berwick strained to speak, but no sound came out. The walker smiled before uttering one word, 'Bye!' and pushed him off. Berwick slid backwards over the scree until his head hit a rock and his body turned sideways rolling down to the distant tarn below. The walker checked no-one was in sight through the mist and pulled out a mobile and sent a text. At the summit, the walker used a litre bottle of water to wash the blade of the ice pick clean. Looking to the east a solitary figure of a woman was striding downwards. The OS map showed an alternative way to the west.

As Diana arrived in Threlkeld, a clutch of mountain rescuers stood around an ambulance outside 'The House and Farrier'. Diana cornered one, flashing her warrant card. 'Where's the body?'

'In the ambulance. Dead when we found him. Cuts all over, suspected broken back, battered skull, shredded skin, matted dry blood and no ID on him. We get one or two falls on Sharp Edge every year, all the damage consistent with what we usually see. You should examine the body.'

Easing back the plastic sheet, the face was unrecognisable. Skin torn away, one eye disgorged and dried congealed blood. Diana's hands started shaking, her breaths quickening, her heart pounding fast, feeling she was going to die. She couldn't think at all, lightheaded, dizzy, she collapsed to the ambulance floor. She tried to slow her breathing and the nausea rising in her mouth, waiting for the panic attack to end. The shredded skin on the body took her back to February, the horror and the MI5 man Neil Denver, only four months ago.

It took ten minutes before the panic attack began to subside. She felt chilled, almost paralysed with cold sweats.

A voice called outside the ambulance. 'Are you OK?'

Diana managed to stand. 'How long before we can get the press here.'

'I'll get on to it, should be here within the hour. You can wait in the pub.'

Swirling the larger around the glass, Diana thought back.

The chatter was about a bombing. One date suggested was the PM's visit to the city on February 23rd. She met with Neil Denver, who was the head of the PM's protection detail, expecting an amicable liaison with the City's force. At their first

30

meeting together he laid out a rollcall of suspect names. He was dismissive to the suggestion of arresting them, explaining others may take their place, so they were under twenty-four-hour surveillance. The other surprise was the PM sanctioned the approach, despite the risk to herself. He was dismissive about cancelling other targets on the day, like the premier league game.

'No, for each threat we receive we always have other events at the same time. We can't have the cycle of a threat made followed by multiple cancellations. I leave it to you to beef up their security. They will need to do proper bag checks and all coats should be removed and searched as well.'

Back in her office Diana opened the files Neil Denver gave her, all marked top secret. The three main suspects were, Nazim Khan a car mechanic, Michael Affredi a primary school teacher and Pervez Khalid a junior accountant. All without a criminal record, all born in the UK.

She remembered the blinding light, the blast that threw her backwards. When she woke all was silent, all was black, as if all light were extinguished. The hot, filthy dust was raining all around. Destruction filled her eyes, her mouth, her nose, and the back of her throat. She stared into the pitch-black and felt the stab of terror and a wave of sickness. Some grey light gradually broke through and she could see the burnt, still bodies. A young man, covered in the grey dust, turn towards her, and spoke but her hearing was gone. Blood poured over the young man's forehead into blinking eyes. Her hearing re-emerged to screams and sirens.

Outside The Horse and Farrier, Diana stood in front of a group of local reporters reading a statement.

'Today at 15:30 a body was discovered, by Scales Tarn, below Sharp Edge. The injuries to the body are consistent with a fall from a considerable height. We are appealing for any possible witnesses who may have seen him on the fell. For the moment we still have to treat this as an unexplained death, until an autopsy is completed.'

8

Here Today

July 21st

'Mrs Stewart, I'm DCI Petrou, this is my colleague DC Giles. Can we come in?'

'Is this about my husband?'

'Yes, would be better if we came in.'

Catherine led them down a wood floored hallway of barren magnolia walls, without paintings or adornments. The lounge was equally minimalist, two leather settees, a coffee table, television fixed to the wall. All very tasteful but lacking family photos, nothing to make it feel like a home. A room for its design not for comfort. A drink was offered. Diana shook her head. Steph perched herself on the arm of a burgundy sofa. Diana was trying to size up this woman. She guessed five-foot seven in height, confident, her blonde locks arranged in a bun, attractive face , slim, appearing younger than she was. She could see that she was expensively dressed from the style of the clothes, the crimson silk scarf, and a diamond necklace.

Diana began. 'Your statement was your husband didn't return two days ago. Why delay in reporting him missing?'

'Sometimes he stays the night in The Horse and Farrier. Finishes his walks, has a meal and a drink, I waited all day for him. Tried his mobile, went to voicemail.'

'What was he wearing?'

'He always wears the same walking clothes. The old-fashioned knee length wool, walking trousers, blue socks, some Brasher boots I bought him, a check shirt, a blue fleece.'

'Mrs Stewart, it appears from his injuries that a man fell off Sharp Edge. Identification is difficult from his facial injuries. I'm

33

so sorry to tell you this but your description of his clothes matches what this man was wearing. Does your husband have any other identifying marks?'

Catherine Stewart broke into sobs.

Steph knelt offering consoling hands, 'We do need to ask a few questions. It's procedure.'

They waited for the sobs to subside before Catherine replied. 'If you think something like a tattoo, no and no odd birth marks.'

Steph held a ring in the palm of her hand. 'How about this ring? It has a date inside of August 10th, 1994.'

The sobs turned returned turning into loud cries and they waited till Catherine composed herself again. 'That's Berwick's ring, the date is when we were married. The body is Berwick. I can't believe he was that reckless. I told him before that Sharp Edge was dangerous, people die in the finest of weather.'

'You're a fell walker too.?'

'I leave that to him. I prefer a round of golf. Do excuse me.'

It was five minutes before she returned.

'This is such a shock.'

Steph asked, 'How long have you been married?'

Catherine straightened up in her chair, 'Twenty-five years next month, we were planning a holiday to Rome to celebrate.'

'Where did you meet?'

'We met as students at St Andrews University, by chance, in the University bar and from a shy start, conversation flowed. We were both natives of Edinburgh, both living at home.'

Catherine rested back into the sofa. 'Berwick was studying computing, maths, and engineering, I was studying geography. He was a strange combination of geeky and handsome. He was an avid cyclist and fit, given all the hills of the city, always skinny. A shock of curly red hair, green eyes, and an eager wide smile. He was kind, thoughtful and intelligent, cleverer than me. We fell in love and a year later married and moved into a modest house.'

The tears returned. Steph handed over a tissue. 'How did you come to the Lake District?'

'Berwick did a PHD, and I found employment with the Ordnance Survey. His studies were about Nuclear Energy. He applied for work at Sellafield. We moved here and he's been highly successful.'

Diana interrupted. 'How was your marriage?'

'It was a perfect until two years ago.'

'What happened two years ago?'

'Berwick descended into another place; the annoyance, the frustration of not solving whatever he was researching, brought on depression, which I've had to help him through. You know he is the IT director and Chief Scientist at Sellafield.' There was a pause before Catherine exclaimed, 'Why do you need all this for what was an accident?'

Diana leaned forward. 'Where were you when this happened, we think it was between two and six pm?'

'Why is that relevant?'

'You weren't with him that day?'

'No, I told you not my thing.'

Diana's instinct was she was lying, but not clear why, something about the way she spoke and her whole demeanour. She was running her finger round the rim of her glass of water to centre herself.

Diana pressed on. 'At around one pm another walker saw him walking up Halls Fell Crag with a woman in a cagoul.'

'That's not me; I don't own a cagoul. The woman was another walker he met en route I expect. He was having a day's break. I drove him, dropped him off promising to pick him up in the pub in Threlkeld when he got down, where he liked to have drinks afterwards. If he wanted that.'

'Was he in good spirits?'

Catherine showed real indignation. 'Yes, he seemed fine, he wasn't contemplating suicide if that's your ridiculous suggestion.

We were happy. His work was demanding but he loved his job and enjoyed the fells.'

'An experienced walker, yet in fine weather he still falls.'

Her lips pursed; her cheeks drawn in. 'Detective, I'm guessing you are not from these parts and don't understand the fells. The fells are dangerous, people die in all sorts of conditions and parts like Sharp Edge are dangerous if you lose your concentration. And didn't the weather worsen that day?'

'Mrs Stewart, we have to pose these questions in these cases where no-one has come forward to witness what has happened. Less people were around. If I didn't consider all options, I might be failing in my job. I say again it's a procedure we have to follow.'

'That's as maybe. I lost my husband of twenty-five years, to a stupid accident. I'm struggling with grief. If you don't mind, I'd like you to both leave if there's no more questions.'

'Of course, thank you for your time. Again, condolences on your loss. Here's my card if anything else occurs to you do call me.'

Steph stood up. 'One last question. Who did Mr Stewart report to at Sellafield?'

'Mark French the COO, but that's irrelevant.'

'No, completing the details.'

Sitting in the car outside the house before Diana could say a word, Steph spoke. 'She's not telling us the whole story. I bet there was something false or fake about the tears. Her eyes were crying but the rest of her was rigid. No hand gestures, no body movements. You know what I mean?'

'I do, it all felt wrong.'

'The answer about a happy marriage, why wasn't she indignant? What was that about him being with someone on the fell, you never told me?'

Diana smiled. 'Spur of the moment test. Instinct tells me we have more to unearth, I made that bit up. I may not be from around here and know these fells. I dunno, I can't buy this is an accident not on a day like yesterday.'

'It does happen, not often, it's usually in adverse weather and she's right the weather did change on the fells in the afternoon. Wet up there, but worse low cloud cover, so an accident is more likely. You have to be on Sharp Edge to realise how dangerous it can be if you don't keep your wits about you. I admit after watching her it's ideal to have an open mind on this. Why that last question?'

'A hunch Steph, with these other murders the name Mark French came up. Suspicious, don't you think?'

9

I want to tell you.

July 21st

It was one bedroom flat above the pie shop in Ambleside. Diana did the introductions. 'Thanks for seeing us, Miss Beck, I'm DCI Petrou and this is my colleague DC Giles, we have some questions about Kim Givens.'

Cody flipped back her curly black tresses, unfolded her arms, and offered a handshake. 'You can call me Cody.'

Diana stared at her hand. How do you get such immaculate fingernails, smooth sided to a curved apex? Stuck on of course. Her dark hair was side parted with silver streaks, she wore a stained wool sweater, which rose up when she stretched. Her legs were clothed in shell suit trackies. In the background the soft sound of Dean Martin was crooning about a lost love. Incongruous for a woman of her age, in her twenties or was it early thirties? There were no lines yet on her angular face.

Cody stared at Steph. 'You were a few years below me at school. You stood out. There weren't many blacks but all the guys fancied you.'

Diana ignored the comment, asking for the music to be turned off. Cody reached for a remote to lower the volume. Diana and Steph sat on a dark settee. Cody settled into a comfy armchair. The floor was strewn with toys. The room was dominated by a wide, flat screen TV, with PlayStation and speakers attached. How could she afford all this? Incongruous, like a tramp with a mobile phone. The room had a musty, damp smell in the air and there was a constant clanging noise from the room next door.

'That's Paul. My bairn.'

Reclining in the chair, her blue eyes were focused.

'I'm told you are Kim's best friend, is that right?'

'Not best friend, but mates maybe, ever since primary school. We both suffered gammy parents, at school we were like sisters. We looked out for one another.'

Diana spoke. 'I hate to tell you this, Kim's death wasn't accidental or a suicide, she was murdered.'

Cody couldn't hide the sadness rippling over her face.

'We conducted an autopsy. She was shot. You know anyone who would want her dead?

'No. Nobody, everyone liked her.'

'What about Dan Jetty?'

'Ahh, the boyfriend. Creep but not a killer. He runs a drug business, weed, owt else on request.'

Diana leaned across. 'You don't think a drug dealer could be a killer?'

For the first time Cody shifted, crossed her slim legs, took a breath, and told her tale how they all knew him from being teenagers. They all tried his dope and he was the sole supplier from one pub in Keswick, where they always got in when underage. She claimed she moved on from all that. She sat forward; her hands grasped together.

'I told Kim he was a bastard, rotten through and through. Kim didn't listen. They've been an item for two years. He's been a shit to her, resented her finding her own career. He likes to own people, dominate them. You might think he's small fry, a local dealer, but his business has got bigger with supplies to other cities like Manchester. Don't let the smart clothes, the neat haircut deceive you, he'll be ruthless to stay at the top of his business, but not murder.'

Diana asked how she knew all this.

Cody mumbled 'I can't say' making a gesture with one finger across her tight shut lips.

Steph spoke for the first time. 'What has she told you about her time at Sellafield?'

39

'She loved the job and liked her boss. I think she might have slept with him. Maybe Jetty found out.'

'What's his name?'

'It's Mark, don't know the surname. Some guy over forty, not my thing. She claimed he treated her right; I think that made her decide to finish with Jetty. Kim was lovely, she was slight, like anyone could lift her up, she never uttered a bad word about anyone.'

Diana intervened. 'Is Adam Wilson a friend?'

'He's Mel's dad, we were all the same year at school.'

'Okay, later we may have further questions. Thanks for your help. One more thing, why did you abandon your baby?

Cody's face tightened.

'No answer? When you dumped her at the hospital, there was a toy in the blanket and the fingerprint matched what we have on record, when you were arrested for possession. I am guessing if we do a DNA test it will confirm you are the parent. Who's the father?'

Cody stared back at Diana, hands twitching, teeth clenched. Diana stayed schtum, unmoved, waiting.

'It was just a one-night stand, don't even know the guy. Stupidly I got pregnant. I couldn't afford to get rid of it. I couldn't afford another bairn. Not in this place, you see how I live. I struggle enough with Paul, I panicked when she was born. I thought being at the hospital, she would be OK.'

'And Dan Jetty. Are you one of his dealers?

'I think you should go.'

Diana stood up. 'Social services will want to see you. I don't think you will see any prosecution, but I can't promise. What else haven't you told us?

'Nowt.'

'We'll be in touch.'

As Diana reached the door the volume on the music rose again. She thought she was tough on the outside. That was a false front. She was like one of those pastries, solid on the plate before they crumble into pieces in your hand. Did she register how vulnerable she was?

Cody watched them disappear down the street before making a call.

'The Police have been here; did you hear Kim was murdered? Course I didn't say owt. We need to be careful.'

10

So Real

July 21st

Blackpool took another bite of his sandwich. A dribble of salad cream spilled down the side of his mouth, wiped away with the back of a gloved hand. He showed a confident air of professionalism that made people trust whatever he was saying. He turned Kim onto her side and took a syringe to show them the entry wound. With a saw he had removed the top of her skull. The brain inside was macerated and a single bit fell onto the floor which he picked up and dropped into a tray. Blackpool was usually stoic, practical but standing back he was caught by the terrible thought that his sister was this age. His conclusion, this was a sniper's bullet, almost silent through the air. The wind, the rain are capable of changing its course. The skilled sniper has to take account for that, will wait until the target stands still. Because it's a high velocity bullet, a cavity is caused by the sonic wave radiating out from the bullet, resulting in severe bleeding and hypothermic shock. The entry hole is neat. Death was quick and painful. Travelling at 1000 mph, enough force was delivered to fling a body into the water.

He elevated the head to reveal to Diana the full damage of a destroyed brain. Diana remembered the dismembered bodies and the pathologist at the autopsies after the bombing repeating the question, how was she coping. Back then Diana lied, but inside she felt revulsion and shame.

Blackpool spoke her name three times before Diana took notice 'You see we have two things here Diana. First, we have an expert, silent killer. Pathology wise, this is almost a perfect murder. The evidence at the scene is solely the bullet in her head which has no prints.'

Diana leapt back into focus. 'You said almost.'

'It's a long shot but if we can pinpoint the position of the two boats on the lake, and we know both were standing at the time we can try and triangulate where the shot came from. Didn't you see her out on the lake? Maybe that will leave clues. Adam Wilson's wounds are identical, same bullet, from the same weapon. In my opinion, same killer.'

'That's not a long shot, that's impossible.'

All the hotel doors were identical. Wedgwood blue, featureless, apart from their dull bronze card readers. Anne Manners squeezed the entry card in her right hand, about to follow the arrow and let the card slip into the slot and thought, sod it, she needed to read the cabinet report again. She took her smartphone from her handbag, showing just after eleven and rang her bodyguard. Work as always won out over tiredness.

'Charlie, I'm going down to the lounge, and work there if it's quiet. Meet me at the lift.'

Slouched in a comfy chair, in a secluded corner, she ordered her favourite nightcap, a double Remy Martin. Half-way through the tedious description of another new green energy plan, she eventually noticed Charlie, hovering.

'Minister, there's someone here who wants a word.'

'Charlie I'm busy, send him away.'

'He says he knows you, Minister.'

Anne looked up to peruse the man standing alongside her minder. 'How do I know you?'

'Excuse me. We met at Sellafield. I'm Mark French, the COO, Chief Operating Officer. I took you and others on a tour of the decommissioning work back in March.'

Anne stayed silent. She remembered French, over six foot, in his 40s, swept back dark hair, well-tailored suit, burgundy tasselled loafers and handsome.

'That's OK Charlie, go get a drink at the bar.'

Anne stood offering a handshake. 'Thanks for being circumspect, there are things I don't want Charlie to know.'

Mark responded, 'I heard you were visiting and after all the calls and emails I thought it was a good opportunity to meet again.'

'Would you like a drink?'

Mark sat in the chair next to her. 'A scotch and ice, thank you.'

A slight gesture with her hand beckoned Charlie who dutifully sorted the drink.

'I remember the first time we met Mark. I remember thinking you were evasive about some of the questions we asked. No, evasive is not the right word, circumspect might be more accurate. I'm a politician. I recognise it when I hear it.'

Anne rolled the brandy glass around in her hand and he smiled.

'Was I? Doesn't sound like me.'

'If you want to talk about the Reclaim project, this might not be the best place, too public.'

'No, I just thought it might be a good opportunity to get to know one another better.'

Mark's charm was insidious. Two hours later talk of Sellafield turned to talk of careers, family, and mutual acquaintances. He was from a wealthy, military background and followed his father into the Army. Graduate of Sandhurst and ended his career with the rank of Major. He was proud about his# current role and enjoyed the authority and responsibility. Of course, he leading the project at Sellafield, this was the reason he was sitting opposite her, but what did he genuinely want? What did he think of her? The ambitious working-class girl from Kendal who strived to get to Cambridge. A first at PPE and by forty risen the ranks to be Minister of State for Energy. For a moment, the conversation lulled. Anne finished her drink and stood up offering a handshake.

'Mark, thanks for the company but I really need to go, have an early meeting.'

He offered over his card. 'Look, let'/s arrange a meeting, maybe at Sellafield, there are events in play you need to know about.'

Anne took the card. 'Of course. Call my office. My PA Jane will sort something, but I warn you, it might be a while.'

'Sorry but this should be sooner rather than later and we should involve Neil.'

'You're right, but I must go.'

Anne walked away with Charlie in tow.

Twenty minutes later there was a knock on her room door.

'Who is it?'

'It's Mark, Mark French. I have a document you left on your chair in the lounge.'

Dan Jetty crept into the kitchen, pulled open a drawer, and chose a carving knife with an eight-inch blade. He ran one finger along the edge, blood oozed, perfect. He slipped the knife up his coat sleeve and headed to the lounge. Cody was waiting for him, sitting in a battered armchair, devouring chocolates, leaving a brown smear on her upper lip. Five vodkas induced in her a foolish bravado. She spat words out at him. 'Give me money in return for not telling on you to the police. All about your relationship, all about the things you did to Kim. You are a prime suspect.'

Jetty towered over her, so she could smell the beer on his breath. 'You are not going to tell nobody.'

'Why is that?'

He smiled placed one knee on to her chest and made a cut down the side of her cheek. Cody screamed and blood dripped down onto her blouse. Fear shivered through her body. She put one hand over the wound.

'I won't say owt.'

'You won't, if you do next time, it won't be you, I hurt, it will be the bairn. Get out.'

11

I'm only sleeping.

July 22nd

Faria Engel propped herself up on one elbow. The bastard was still sleeping. Why did she spend another night with him? The initial lust and illicit thrill were gone. The swine was handsome with those deep-set brown eyes that gazed at her with such intensity. Women did stare at him, caught by the physique he retained from years in the Army, six feet, toned, strong and the permanent tanned skin. He never showed a wide smile, it was always, she felt, a sly grin.

She whispered in his ear, 'Du bist eine scheisse!'

She clambered out of the bed, picking their discarded clothes off the floor as she went, fumbling around the debris of phones and hotel literature until she found the packet of cigarettes. Lighting up, taking the first saving drag, she glanced at herself in the mirror. At thirty-three, the running kept her body trim, and a few lines showed around her dark green eyes. She thought to herself, I'm desirable, I deserve better than this. Why did she fall in with men who deemed themselves protectors but were controllers? She shook him hard.

Mark French rolled onto his back, his eyes blinking as they adjusted to the light.

'It's seven already, Mark I've gotta leave and get to work before you. I'll chase down Berwick. He should have been back from his walking yesterday; we can't progress without him.'

In the bathroom, she turned on the shower. Mark shouted after her. 'Well if you are not staying, I have a favour you can do for me today.'

Faria stuck her head back round the bathroom door. 'What?'

'If you are not staying you can do me a favour today.'

47

'What is it? We are already behind schedule; without Berwick we can't catch up.'

Mark shouted at the bathroom door. 'I've got a policewoman coming to see me from Windermere at 6:00pm, a DCI Petrou, to enquire about Kim's murder I expect. I'm far too busy to spend time with her. You speak to her and find what she's after.'

'How do I do that?'

'Use your imagination.'

'If I refuse.'

The reply was predictable. 'When's your next promotion review?'

'You are a scheisse.'

The descent down Wrynose Pass into Seascale was steep, working hard the VW's brakes. For once it was a bright day of blue skies, in the distance the coastline and Irish Sea. Diana switched off the music, to think through handling Mark French. Now, all roads seem to lead to him. The phone rang.

'Diana, it's Blackpool, got an interesting finding for you.'

'Can't it wait. I'm heading over to Sellafield.'

The voice crackled through a three-bar reception.

'You need to hear this before you get to Sellafield. I've done more tests on Wilson. It's what I found on the body.'

The signal died. Round a blind corner a SUV came straight towards the VW. Diana slammed the brakes and pulled to the side. The SUV passed by without any acknowledgement. Four hundred yards on was a layby to pull in to. What the hell was Blackpool pestering her for this time? He seemed competent enough, a prejudice stayed, lurking, that he was a pathologist in a backwater, without experience or facilities.

She redialled on the phone. 'I lost the signal, a bastard almost banged into me. I'll never get used to this road. OK, what is it? Don't be wasting my time.'

Blackpool chuckled. 'Who's upset you, Steph again? I've examined the body of Wilson again and it's what I've detected.

I worked on a hunch. Wilson shows exposure to radiation and around here there's only one place that could have happened. You ever been told he was on site?'

'No, I haven't, that doesn't show in any of his records. Begs the question, what work was he doing and why is it a secret? Thanks that's useful.'

'There's a message from Steph too. She looked through Kim Given's Instagram site, lots of pictures of her and Jetty and in some, guess who, Adam Wilson and his son. Also found in her phone a picture she took of a computer screen. It's an email addressed to The Minister of Energy, Anne Manners from Mark French, all about something called Reclaim which needed construction work at Sellafield and Givens sent it to Adam Wilson. I'm guessing he was involved in that work. But that does connect them both together. Steph's going to interview Adam Wilson's son.

12

Across the great divide

July 22nd

Steph banged on the warehouse wooden door, until it was answered by a squat, overweight young man in blue overalls, with unkempt red hair and an acne pitted face. The accent was broad Cumbrian. Steph flashed her warrant card. Mel Wilson ushered her in. The office wreaked of stale food and cold coffee. The wooden shelf along one side was a mess of piles of papers with hanging clip boards. At the desk was one old-fashioned wooden, revolving, slatted chair.

Steph cleared away a pile of newspapers to sit down on the only other chair. 'Mr Wilson, I am sorry for your loss. To find your father's killer there's answers to questions that could help us with our enquiries.'

Mel Wilson was impassive, settled into the desk chair.

Steph carried on. 'Were you living at home with your father?'

'No, I left a few months ago, I've got rooms in North Street in Ambleside. I don't intend to be rude but no-one has told me what happened, why is it all secret, why a post-mortem? All I know is that his body was found washed up on the lake. How did he die?'

Steph explained. 'That's why we are here. I can now tell you it wasn't an accident. Your father was murdered, he was shot whilst out on the lake. That's all we know.'

'What!'

Mel swivelled the chair away lowering his head into his hands. The words flowed in annoyance. 'First, I lose the father I cared for, now you tell me he was murdered. This is ludicrous.

He's a reputable businessman, we have a father and son construction business.'

'I can see this is a shock. I promise you we will find the killer. We are hoping a post-mortem might tell us more about when he was killed, the bullet and gun used. Has he been threatened, anyone he has crossed doing business?'

Mel regained his composure and turned back. 'I don't get this. Always a few disgruntled customers, usual for our business, nothing that you'd kill over. That's ludicrous. We do have our own yacht which he went out in, his way of relaxing, getting away from the business, straight after work. If he was shot, are you saying it might be a person he knows well, in the yacht with him? It was kept at Low Wood Marina. Where he parked his Audi too.'

Steph switched tack. 'You are sure, some businesses you may have crossed?'

'None. I can't think of anyone. You should go see my younger sister, she helps run the business, does the books, works part-time at the climbing shop in town. In fact she is in the process of applying to join the Police.'

At that moment, the phone rang. Steph took the chance to walk over and peruse the names on the clip boards. Each included an invoice. One in particular caught her eye. Headed paper from Sellafield. Before she could see any details or names, Mel turned back towards her.

Steph spoke. 'I'll leave you. We will be in touch to do a formal identification. I will keep you informed on our investigation. One last thing, do you know Kim Givens?'

'Kim, yes, we were at school in the same class, haven't seen her much since, why?'

'Kim died on the 12th. Maybe nothing. She was shot too. Have you any dealings with her boyfriend Don Jetty?'

'That scumbag. I don't spend my time with low-lifes like that, he hangs out in Keswick. He was a shit at school, still a shit.'

Steph stood shook Mel's hands, gave him her business card.

'By the way where were you again the afternoon or later the 15th.'

Mel shouted back. 'I was at a customer in Keswick all afternoon. I can give you the company name, they will tell you I was there all the time.'

'In the evening?'

'Went home, got a takeaway, watched tele, went for a pint in The Unicorn. OK?'

'That's fine. Sorry again for your loss.'

As Steph walked out of the warehouse she thought, must get those alibis checked and why did he pretend he didn't know Kim was murdered? The story and her picture were on the front page of the newspaper she took off the office chair. What were they doing at Sellafield?

It was a moment before Diana become aware she'd been joined on the bench by a woman lighting a cigarette. One eye was hidden by her mahogany brown, wavy tresses flowing over one shoulder. She turned towards Diana. 'Do you mind if I smoke?'

Diana shrugged her shoulders. 'No, that's fine.'

For a few minutes both of them resumed staring out over the lawns at the people streaming out of the Sellafield's main building before the silence was broken. 'Hi, I'm Faria, I haven't seen you here before. Which department are you in?'

They shook hands.

'I don't work here. I'm DCI Diana Petrou here for a meeting with Mark French your COO, I got here quicker than I planned. I thought why not sit out in the sunshine.'

Faria broke into a smile before explaining Mark was her boss and guessed the meeting to be about Kim Givens. 'That was tragic, we hear she was murdered, is that right?'

Diana was already making assumptions guessing, she was mid-30s, dressed in a black pinstripe, pencil skirt, shaped white shirt with blue trimming around the collar and cuffs. Lightly applied make up, black designer watch, gold necklace, and no wedding ring.

'Did you and Kim socialise?'.

'Not outside of this place, only at arranged meetings, trips, shared lunches. Mr French rated his PA, he trusted her.'

Diana's mobile rang. She walked away a few paces. Faria could hear the gist of the conversation; it was obvious that Mark planned to put her off, suggesting a morning meeting.

'Has Mark let you down?'

'Yes, an unannounced visit from an MP. What's your role here?'

'I manage all the major current projects. Or rather I try to control a bunch of scientists smarter than me. My role is to keep them on track and sticking to the budget.'

'That sounds demanding. I guess in that role you get to befriend people here, being in proximity to your boss. I don't want this to be a wasted journey on my part, could we talk about Kim, it might be valuable?'

'I guess I'm free, how about a drink and a bite to eat. I'm starving, haven't eaten all day, a decent pub is a five-minute walk away with a sheltered garden to sit in.'

Two hours later they were sitting in the twilight outside the Stanley Arms sharing a second bottle of Sauvignon Blanc. There was something in the way she talked about French that made Diana think there was something more between them.

'Tell me,' Diana said, 'How long have you been here.'

'Five years now, I came over from Germany where I trained at a nuclear installation. My mother was Turkish, came to Germany and met my father. They were both academics and at the University in Heidelberg as lecturers, so Germany is my real home. I'll go back sometime.'

Diana interrupted. 'I didn't clock the time. Doesn't seem worth driving back. Can you suggest places to try for a room for the night?'

Handing over her phone, 'Try a couple of these, but we have a conference going on, you might be unlucky.'

Two phone calls later and the answer was no vacancies.

'Look Diana, I feel awful Mark has let you down. I have a spare room at my apartment, save you a night journey over the passes.'

'Are you sure, I don't want to put you out.'

'It's the least we can do, it's no problem.'

In the morning, Faria slipped on her dressing gown and walked down the corridor to the spare room with a cup of coffee. The room was empty except for a note on the pillow saying thank you. She made a call.

13

Here there and everywhere.

July 23rd

Faria pushed the contracts and pen across the desk.

'Mark, can you get a new PA appointed. I've other urgent work to get back to.'

Before he could answer his desk phone rang.

'Is that Mark French.'

'Yes, who's this?'

'Neil Denver from MI5. I've taken over security on the Reclaim project. Are you alone?'

'Stop. First your call has come out of the blue. You could be anyone. So I should end this call now.'

'You are completely right. Go off the call, google MI5 phone number. Millbank in London. Call back and ask to be put through to me.'

Two minutes later, Neil answered. 'Hello Mark. Glad you didn't take me on my word. Are you alone?'

'No.'

'Whoever's there can you send them out of the room.'

Mark dismissed Faria with a flick of his fingers. Faria headed straight to Kim's desk, sat behind the barrier, gently lifted the receiver, and pushed a button to listen in.

'Now what's this about?

'Things are moving at a pace since Mr Stewart's accident. Thankfully, I presume you are aware that he finished his research successfully and we have a full working solution for Reclaim. We are moving on from the whole verification process and have chosen some specialist scientists to do the work. The challenge is to keep it secret, so we are sequestering them at GCHQ. At

Sellafield we only want you to know what's going on. Am I clear? Inside the Government only the PM and Anne Manners knows the plan for revenue generation. The agreement with you stand as promised as long as there's no hiccups. Confirm to me, nobody else at Sellafield knows about this, everyone thinks it's only decommissioning going on.'

Mark only uttered one word. 'Confirmed.'

'We have a cover story being prepared to explain the need for new construction at the site. Now tell me. Are you still sleeping with our Minister, Anne Manners.'

'Pardon, what are talking about?'

'Mark, bodyguards have more loyalty to us than to their Ministers. It's not a problem, in fact maybe really helpful in keeping tabs on her and what she knows.'

Faria stifled a curse, mouthing a few profanities before going back to the call.

Mark was curt. 'That's my private life and none of your business.'

'Let's be clear. Whilst all this is going on, everything is my business. If you don't like that we can find you another place to go. Do you understand?'

There was silence down the phone.

'Do you understand.'

'Yes.'

'I will be coming up soon. By the way have you met a DCI Petrou?'

Mark gathered himself again. 'No, but she's due here later today. She wants to talk about my PA Kim Givens who was murdered. There's a rumour running round there may be a serial killer on the loose.'

'I read about this. Look, I've met her before. She's really smart, so careful what you say and she will ask about Berwick too. The story has to be he was leading some of the actions on the decommissioning, nothing else. Whatever you do, keep the story straightforward. I'll be in touch.'

The call went dead. Faria waited for Mark to put his receiver down.

The stylish chenille settee was designed for maximum discomfort. Her knees were so low down they were level with her midriff. The visitor centre reception was square and sparse. She was more interested in the comings and goings through the marbled atrium. A mixture of men in suits or white lab coats strolling through the gentle swish of the automatic gates into security scanners familiar from airports. The security guards uniform displayed the name of government's favourite outsourcer, full of ex-coppers.

She picked up a brochure browsing until she got to page ten showing a picture of Mark French. He was tall, smiling, with thick dark hair, maybe in his forties. The article detailed Sellafield's history, its cost of one hundred and twenty-one billion over twenty years, and its redundant technology. Bored she picked up a copy of Cosmopolitan, with a tale of a woman using strangers to get pregnant. The receptionist called her over. It was an effort to stand up.

'Mr French will see you now, make your way to the security desk.' Diana emptied the contents of her jackets and trousers into a grey plastic tray, walking through the scanner.

To her surprise on the other side she was met by Faria.

'I didn't expect to see you. Thanks for last night, I woke early, decided to get up to do my mail. I am grateful for the hospitality.'

Faria smiled. 'I was ready to help out. Follow me to the lifts.'

At the top floor it was a brief walk to a frosted glass door, which Faria pushed open.

'Mark, you free, this is DCI Petrou?'

Mark French came out from behind his desk handshake at the ready. From his height, his build, and unblinking stare, Diana already felt he was trying to dominate.

'Pleased to meet you. I apologise about yesterday. It's been manic here at the moment. I'm on a constant meeting schedule of visitors. Coffee?'

'White no sugar, thanks.'

Fiddling with a fancy new machine, favoured by George Clooney, he asked, 'Is this your first visit here.'

'Yes. I'm not a local, here on secondment. You been here long?'

'Five years now. Perfect place for me, I'm a keen fell walker, been coming here since I was a teenager, first with my father, later with Army buddies.'

He handed over a coffee and they both sat down.

'Army?'

'Yes, joined when I was eighteen, went through officer training at Sandhurst, following Father's footsteps. Served till 2014, and decided this was the area to live, applied for a job at Sellafield where they seemed to think my Army skills were relevant. Climbed the greasy pole to COO. That's the abbreviated version. What about you?'

Diana took a swig of coffee. 'Different, always been in the police. I joined when I was seventeen, passed exams, made a DC began my climb up the greasy poll, to DCI. In the Police you go where they send you. They needed a DCI here. Proper break for me. I'm getting into the fell walking.'

French broke into a broad smile. 'Isn't it wonderful. Though I do prefer scary places like Lord's and Jakes Rake, Striding Edge, Sharp Edge.'

Diana put up her hand. 'Sharp Edge, where your colleague Berwick died.'

French sank back in his chair, gripping the desk. 'Yes, Berwick Stewart, my leading scientist,' shaking his head, 'Bloody tragic. He will be missed. You must be careful what you are doing. People die in the fells every year.'

Diana took a moment to gauge French's posture, body language, demeanour, was he showing any notion of grief? 'We have an autopsy to do and reaching out for any witnesses to see when it happened and how he fell. The weather worsened that day.'

'Do let me in on any developments but I presume you have come about Kim Givens.'

'As you probably know from the news, it's now a murder enquiry. There's a few questions.'

He heard what happened and explained she was a talented girl and was his PA for two years. To his knowledge she didn't seem to have any enemies or anybody with a grudge against her. He didn't share about her private life, the one thing he knew was that she was an only child and lived with her mother in Ambleside. To Diana it was like a prepared speech, faultless words, he sat upright, hands resting on the arms of his chair.

'Are you saying you learnt nothing of your own PA's private life, that you don't care about her relationships.'

The response was brusque. 'No, I don't. It's a policy of mine to not care, I like the separation of business and personal, far better that way. I'm not interested in gossip; I like to focus on the job.'

Diana folded her arms, this didn't wash. 'I can appreciate that with other employees, but she was your PA, in that role, she must have known about your life in making all the arrangements for you. Is it credible you knew nothing of hers?'

French showed the first signs of true irritation, his hands gripped tight together. 'Well I don't and that's that. I have found it it's much better to stick to business. To find out about her life chat to those who socialised with her, try Faria. All I can tell you is in the last couple of months she was fine here, she seemed happy enough doing her job.'

'Did you notice any change in her behaviour the last few weeks, any unexplained absences?'

'No, nothing, it was all business as usual. Do you have any evidence about who did this?'

'Not at the moment, but we have several lines of inquiry. Did she ever mention to you the name, Dan Jetty?'

'Not that I recall, who's he?'

'Just a boyfriend.'

French stood up. 'If there's nothing else, I do have another meeting scheduled, but keep me informed and if there's anything else I can do to help let me know.'

Diana didn't budge. 'One last thing, did she have access to sensitive, secure information.'

'She did, but like everyone else who does, she signed the official secrets act. What we are involved in now is public knowledge, the decommissioning, in that sense we have nothing secret happening. I'm already late for my next meeting, Faria will show you out.'

Outside the building Diana felt pleased that she got him annoyed and knew he wasn't telling the whole story.

Driving back over Wrynose Pass, she remembered Steph's comment about it in the dark. The corridors of shadowing fells, hairpin bends with precipitous drops either side, the brakes burning. She preferred it in the morning light. Her brain was also trying to fathom what she learnt from French. An ambiguity about the man was obvious, with that real air of self-confidence. The pictures on the wall showed he was ex-army, and the accent was home counties, a public-school boy she bet. What she heard was either obstruction or downright fallacies. Distracted, Diana snapped back in time after a van came around a bend. She swerved, brakes crying till coming to a halt. Her hands tightened on the steering wheel the panic was beginning. She sat motionless for ten minutes before normality returned. Forty minutes later she walked into her office.

Steph was sitting with her feet up on her desk. 'You're late Di, where were you last night?

'First, I stayed over, second, get out from my desk, third, get me a coffee.'

Steph eased herself up. 'First, check, second check, third for the umpteenth time, get your own. Another rough night again?'

'No choice I stayed over, couldn't see Mark French till this morning.'

Steph plonked herself on the opposite side of the desk and took a container from her bag.

Diana grimaced at the smell. 'What are you eating?'

'Prunes.'

'Ullgh, disgusting, soggy prunes.'

Steph managed to chew and talk at the same time. 'Changing the subject, where did you stay?'

Diana fiddled with her papers. 'Hotels were full, a conference going on, I accepted the offer of a room from one of their execs, Faria Engel. She reports to Mark French, took the opportunity too, after he blew me out, to get more background on him and Kim Givens. My instincts tell me she was equivocating, nowhere near the truth in our conversations. I'd hazard a guess that her and French are in a relationship.'

Pushing the prunes to one side, Steph perched on the desk. 'Let's see, it was a pure accident she met you and ended offering you a room? Di, I have a thought. Did you have your tablet, your phone with you? Let me see.'

After five minutes of typing, Steph passed both back with a troubled expression. 'Unless you were up in the middle of the night, your phone and tablet were both accessed at 3:30am by a person who knows what they are doing. Read your files, your emails about Givens, Wilson, and Stewart. Respectfully, you're a daft apeth, 1234 is not a password.'

Diana tilted her head to one side in a reluctant admission. 'Steph gleam what you can about her. Her mother is Turkish but emigrated to Germany, married a German and she was born and brought up there. Find out when she arrived here and her job background. Whatever she is doing it's at French's behest. He gave little away when I quizzed him. A picture on his wall showed him in the Army with the insignia of a Major. But despite that, I still feel it in my bones that we have a serial killer. The other possibility is this is all Jetty's doing. Maybe he's not the insignificant low life we thought. Maybe he's hired a killer to do the shootings. If that's the case, is it a reason to kill Wilson? Was he part of his drug business? What's the motive for killing Givens? Jealousy or does she hold a secret of his? Was he scared she might speak out? We think it is the same killer. Maybe she found papers in his place or overheard a conversation. Here's a thought, could Wilson be part of his supply chain, drugs coming in hidden in his business shipments?'

Steph held up both hands. 'Di, take a breath. Look if Jetty were behind this, I still find it hard to believe that he would have Givens killed because she dumped him. For Wilson, there might be a purpose in killing him if he was trying to take over the business or taking a bigger cut. We've also found out that days before the murders, Jetty made a trip to Dublin for some reason.'

'We have a myriad of pieces in motion, but I don't yet get the pattern. The Sellafield connection is where French isn't telling us everything. Why get the woman to go through my stuff?'

The rest of the intended monologue was disturbed by Martins striding in, waving a paper. 'Ma'am, I've got a suspect. He's an ex-Army man, member of a gun club, they tell me he's a crack shot. They have an annual competition, for handguns and bigger weapons. He always wins.'

'Well?' Diana exclaimed, 'The name you idiot!'

Martins flipped through a few pages. 'Here it is. John Castle, he was a corporal, served in Afghanistan, retired. He's 48. Not married, bit of a loner, lives in Grasmere.'

'Right, more inquiring on his background, any Army contacts to find, any family. We will pay a surprise visit.'

14

Bad man's song

July 24th

They stood outside a 19th century terraced house, with a neat front garden and dark green front door. Giles wrapped on the gold, lion knocker. The door opened, on a chain.

Steph flashed her warrant card. 'Mr Castle?'

'Yes, what do you want?'

'Just a few questions. We would you like to come to the station with us.'

Castle grimaced. 'I don't want to go to your station. You have questions, ask them now.'

'We would like to do that, but we have some items and pictures to show you that might help with our enquiries. It's not an interview, we just need some help.'

'I was about to go out.'

'Mr Castle.'

Castle walked away leaving the door on its chain. Steph turned to Di.

'Can you go round the back in case he does a runner.'

'That's one suggestion, I'll stay here you go round the back.'

About to debate the matter, John Castle emerged from the door and walked out, dressed in all black walking gear and a full length, grey duffle coat.

The ten-minute car journey was in complete silence. The first words he spoke were in interview room one, to confirm his name and address.

It was one of the strangest interviews Diana ever conducted. At first, they left him alone for five minutes, observing him from outside the room. He was a broody, hulk of a man. Solid shoulders, over six foot and hands that Diana imagined could strangle a man. His head was shaved, with a curved jaw line to a pointed chin. He sat bolt upright, his right foot twisting on the floor. There was an air of both menace and calm. In another life, a bodyguard, or a cage fighter. Diana interviewed so many criminals in the last twenty-five years and learnt to trust her first impressions. There was no doubt, this man could kill.

Diana sat directly opposite Castle. Steph stood in the corner. Diana laid her folder out before going through the usual introductions. Her approach in interviews was usually the same. She didn't go for bluster or outbursts. She directed questions, staring straight at the interviewee, and played on silence.

Steph asked the first question. 'Mr Castle, related to a recent event, we are talking to everyone who is a member of the local gun club. You are a member, yes?'

Castle simply nodded and eventually spoke slowly with no inflection.

'What event? What's this about?'

The voice matched the man, a resonant bass.

Di cut in. 'Someone was shot on Lake Windermere. You may have seen the news. We are asking for any help in identifying the killer. It was a skilled shot, over five hundred metres, would you know anyone at the Gun Club capable of such a shot.'

For the first time Castle smiled. 'Yes, me. But I didn't do this. And before you go any further, I am sure you have checked my background and found I was in the Army. I left a few years ago and came here for peace and quiet. I live alone, keep myself to myself, so before you ask, I probably have no alibi. But I didn't do this.'

'Do you own a Rifle?'

'No, I don't, I only use the weapons provided at the Gun Club.'

The series of questions that followed were all met with an obstinate silence or an occasional, no comment. Until asking about his time in the Army.

'I joined at eighteen, served in Ireland, the Balkans and Afghanistan.'

'Weren't you trained as a sniper?'

The stern gaze lightened into a smile for the first time. 'I was only a corporal, not a role they gave me.'

Steph interrupted. 'Isn't that role down to skill, not rank?'

'Check my record.'

'Why did you leave the Army before your contracted time?

That was his last words. He stayed obstinately silent to any questions about his family, social life or where he was on the morning of the two murders.

Di's phone rang, she listened without comment.

'Mr Castle I have to tell you we have checked with the Army and you were indeed trained as a sniper. I also have to tell you that we have a warrant to search your house and found bullets and a rifle. Why have you got those?'

As always, a single word answer.

'Hunting.'

Diana laid her hands on the table. 'What do you hunt?'

'Rabbits, Pheasant.'

Steph laid a piece of paper on the table. 'You should see this.'

Diana made satisfactory noises, reading it before turning and pushing the paper over to Castle.

'You didn't resign your service; you were dishonourably discharged after a friendly fire incident in Afghanistan. You were a sniper, held responsible for shooting an American soldier. The definitive finding describes you as unstable. Mr Castle, have you been angry, did you kill Kim Givens and Adam Wilson? Both were shot by a trained man with the skills and the weapons to kill from a distance. That's you, isn't it?'

Castle's hands pushed strongly against the edge of the table, staring back.

'You don't have any proof I committed these crimes, nothing to tie me to them. I am an expert shot but so are many others. I was discharged, but that didn't turn me into a psychopath. I made

65

a mistake. I regret it. I like to live alone, to be in the shelter of the fells. I will make it clear. I did not, repeat not, kill these two people and I won't be interviewed by you again till you can show some real evidence.'

'Mr Castle, we have enough circumstantial evidence to keep you here for questioning and allow you to contact legal assistance.'

Before they could respond, Castle stood and drew an automatic from inside his coat and pointed it straight at Steph's head.

'Over here!'

He grabbed Steph around the throat walking backwards to the door. Di went to approach him.

'Stay where you are. Remember I'm a crack shot.'

At the end of the narrow corridor, he tightened the grip on Steph's throat.

'Put in the code and slowly push the door.'

In reception Sergeant Collins was at the desk. 'Open the front door. You hesitate she dies.'

The double doors swung inwards and they walked outside.

'Detective, give me your car keys.'

Steph pulled them from her jeans pocket. Castle, pressed the remote and the taillights of a blue Audi flashed a short way down, parked amongst a group of Police cars. He opened the boot and threw Steph in and drove out of the station, gravel flying in his wake. Ten minutes later outside Windermere, he pulled over and released the boot.

'Out, it's your lucky day.'

The Audi disappeared up the A91. Steph screaming after the speeding car.

An hour later in the Wansfell Arms, they both knocked a brandy in one gulp. Diana thumped the table and covered her face with her hands as she spoke. 'Hell. Why didn't we search him? I've got lax since coming here. And you could have been killed. I'm so sorry Steph.'

'No, it's down to me as well. Let's talk about what we do next. We now have a genuine suspect for our serial killer. I phoned in an APB and got Martins looking again at background. There should be a photo from the Gun Club registration that we can circulate. I'll check if we can find any possible link to Givens or Wilson, everything in that room tells me we have a psychopath, who likes shooting people.'

Diana tapped the desk. 'I agree but let's not put all our eggs in one basket just yet. We can go to Givens mother again and Mel Wilson. Remember maybe there's other motives, like our friend Mr Jetty. And what if it's not a serial killer but Castle was hired to shoot these people. We do now need to contact all the media and let them know we have a dangerous man on the run, not to be approached and maybe linked to the killings on Windermere.'

'To borrow from you, let's rattle the cages. Let's bring Jetty in. Let's question some others, make a show of bringing them in, like his mother, that woman Cody, Mel Wilson and known dealers. Get him tailed, put the frighteners on his usual customers. Let the press have the story we are concerned about drugs in Cumbria. Hint that it all maybe connected. We can see how he copes.'

'Steph. You are right, we've been too light footed. I suppose Ingles will object; he'll be convinced it's Castle, convinced he's our serial killer and nothing else. Get Martins to go through all Adam Wilson's contracts, all his business contacts, his accounts.

'One other thing Di. There's still the dead man on Blencathra. We should interview that Mrs Stewart again.'

It was a starry night and Diana was focused on the full moon in reflected fragments on the rippled surface of Windermere. Stretching back in her wicker chair, she savoured the exquisite taste of a glass of Rioja. She swirled the liquid round the bowl of the glass, admiring its colour through the lamplight, before taking another mouthful. She knew she should have eaten. The sole content of the fridge was the remnants of a curry, not an acceptable accompaniment. The wine eased the pain and anxiety. Two murders and a serial killer suspect with little forensic evidence. She resorted to drink to encourage sleep.

Later as her eyelids were closing, the mobile rang. She let it ring through to voice mail. The cheery voice this late was Blackpool's. 'Get yourself to Autopsy. Ring me back.'

Diana fumbled for her phone amongst the debris of notes. 'What is it, it's after ten. Can't this wait till tomorrow?'

'No, it's from the autopsy on Berwick Stewart, you have to see the results. It will change what you say to the press conference tomorrow.'

'Alright, I'm tipsy, this better be worthwhile. I'll have to get a taxi, be with you as soon as I can.

The pungency of disinfectant and formaldehyde announced autopsy before Di entered through the automatic double doors, pacing across the scrubbed white tiles. Only one of the six tables for the dead was occupied. Blackpool and Steph were waiting beside a body.

'Blackpool, what's that you're holding?'

'My usual, ham and homemade piccalilli sandwich, they're delicious.'

Blackpool wafted it under Diana's nose, before taking a bite. 'It's finest Cumbrian ham and Jane's homemade piccalilli.' A sliver of which dribbled out of one corner of his mouth.

'Blackpool, let's get on with this.'

'Alright. What have you heard about Sharp Edge?' Diana shook her head, 'Sharp Edge is the quickest, most dangerous route off the summit of Blencathra. It's a thirty-degree slope downwards over jagged rocks, with a three hundred-foot, sheer drop, each side. It's famous amongst walkers, a familiar rite of passage to test your nerve. Most years an unlucky climber dies there.'

Blackpool took another bite of the sandwich, more bits of piccalilli dripped onto his white plastic overall and turned to Diana. 'My slightly inebriated DCI, an autopsy lesson. I've dealt with falls off the fells, including Sharp Edge. Come over and examine our dear departed corpse.'

Diana and Steph watched on as Blackpool pulled back the black sheet. It was a sight Diana remembered, an unrecognisable face, with skin ripped off, below a broken skull and layers of dried blood that turned her stomach, with a decaying smell. The body was a mess of cuts and bruises. The skin was shredded, ingrained with dirt. Steph felt her nausea rise. Blackpool pointed to a bin, sighed, ignored the retching, breathed out and pronounced. 'DCI Petrou this body did not fall by accident.'

'How the hell can you tell, with it in this state?'

'Because of this.'

Blackpool, always one for the theatrics, manoeuvred the body over onto its front and with arms outstretched like a conductor. 'Because of this.'

Blackpool pointed with his pen, 'In the back of his head there's a single, perfectly rectangular indentation several inches deep.'

Diana interrupted, 'From his head being bashed on the rocks?'

'No! The chances of making a regular hole like this are impossible. He's been struck from behind, with tremendous force. From the shape of the hole if you look at it with the magnifier, the bottom has minute, regular, serrated indentations. I'm guessing the weapon was something like a small ice pick, I can't think of anything else that you might have up a fell making that shape. That killed him on its own, without the fall, as it has gone all the way through to his brain. After that he slid mostly front first all the way down to the tarn, hence less damage on his back. I'm guessing the killer thought any traits would be wiped out with him careering down that rockface.'

Blackpool paused. 'Diana, Steph, this was murder. Coffee?'

'Steph, I think a proper drink is in order.'

Diana trailed behind Steph walking up North Road feeling the troubling silence. She was surprised the horrors of Stewart's body and that the sight of the mutilated head didn't bring on an attack. For Steph it was her first and the images would be irremovable. Diana pulled on Steph's arm. She turned, anguish imprinted on her face, breathing fast, shaking.

Di hugged her. 'I can't say it will get better. You'll find your own way to deal with it.'

'Will I? Is this something I want to deal with.'

Still shaking, Diana held her hands. 'Would it help to talk?'

'Let's get a drink at the pub at the top of the road. By the way, Martins rang, they found my car. We are assuming he's stolen another car or maybe caught a bus. We've searched the house, there's no weapons there now.

'Maybe he has a hiding place we didn't find. God help us if he has another weapon.'

They strode on side by side. Steph spoke. 'Our dead man, Berwick Stewart, in Autopsy. When we did the routine search of his house, and this is strange for a scientist, we couldn't find a laptop, tablet or phone.'

'Maybe he kept it safe at his lab?'

'The wife claimed he always brought those home and kept them locked in their safe. I think someone may have gotten to it before us.'

The Unicorn was an English pub cocooned in the 1930s, stained dark brown floorboards, yellowing walls from years of cigarette smoke plus the inevitable line of older men propped against the bar. It smelt of polish, beer, and decay.

Diana shoved her way through to the bar to order two lagers, whilst Steph searched for the toilet. Looking in the mirror she saw an ashen, desperate face. When she closed her eyes all she saw was a face without any skin. She felt convulsions starting in her stomach, an acidic taste in her throat before she vomited into the sink and collapsed to the floor crying.

A voice broke through the sobbing. 'Steph are you OK?'

It was a familiar face of an old friend. It took consistent breaths to stammer out,

'I'll be OK. It'll be OK.' Giving out a long sigh, 'It's been a tough day.'

'Come on, let me get you up, I'll get you a drink. Let's get your favourite Vodka. Tell me what's wrong.'

At the other end of the bar Diana was swilling back the lager. Her thoughts were on the murders. They didn't make sense. The first two murders were clean shots from a distance, impersonal. Berwick's was close up and personal. This didn't match a serial killer profile. We have two killers. Why empty out his house? Steph was in conversation at the other end of the bar. Diana mouthed, I'm off, downed the lager and strode out.

No matter how Steph tried the front door it always creaked. She eased it shut. Her coat slipped off the stand. She was too weary to pick it up, feeling infected from the sights of the last days. Two dead bodies shot through the head, one murdered on a fell. Sod it, she thought, and went to the loo. A perfect spot to pee and calm down.

Sauntering into the lounge, Martine was dozing, splayed out on the settee, her legs curled up into a protective ball. Her straight black tresses hid half her face. Big Ben was chiming for the midnight news. Steph squatted down and lifted the dark strands.

'Hi there, you didn't need to wait up.'

Martine smiled. 'Was watching a film and fell asleep.'

Steph threw her badge on the table. 'I'm happy to be home back to the comfort of this place.'

Martine sat up, staring intently. 'That bad?'

'Yeh, it's been a shit day. Some days are depressing, have to keep reminding myself, this is the job I'm suited for, the job where I can do well, a job that's worthwhile.'

Martine hugged her gently and Steph spoke over her shoulder. 'There's three murders now and we're not trying to take down the worst local drug lord. Not your normal day. I'm shattered. I'm off to bed, good night.'

In the bathroom, Steph stared into the mirror, taking off the day's make-up from one of her two faces.

15

The promised land

July 25th

The sniper counted them, there were eighty-two. It was a dangerous indulgence to record each kill, but a way to relive each glorious moment. Not some gruesome nostalgia, not merely brushing off the cobwebs. The postcard for some was another casualty of the digital age, a relic, like the handwritten letter. But he loved the images, to touch and feel the past. He satisfied himself cataloguing in different ways, chronologically, by age and by location. Three postcards for each event, in three different albums.

He found albums where you can display both sides, the picture, and the words. On the words side, his own code of the target, place, weapon, bullet, distance, and the exact position where the projectile entered the body.

He left it to his thoughts only, as he thumbed the albums with protective gloves, which kills were the most satisfying. With each image he felt transported to another world, divorced from normality. He wondered; all these people he killed, could they imagine a country where decency was shredded till only the animal instinct to survive remained. That was Bosnia in 1999. It wasn't a war. Just unleashed historic hatred. He had no regrets for the revenge he perpetrated even though his victims were surrogates for the real villains.

In December 1995 his unit engaged Serbian troops and all but eight were killed who were held prisoner, awaiting transport away from the front line. He stared at them all day, thinking could any of these eight have killed his family in cold blood. He woke before everyone else the next day and told the prisoners

73

that transport was ready and to follow him. When they reached a clearing outside our camp, he told them to get down on their knees. He shot each one in the back of the head, saying the names, one by one, of his slaughtered family as he shot. Looking up, his commander was watching him through it all and never intervened.

He persuaded the army to train him as a sniper, to carry on his vengeance. After his first kills, it was clear he could dispatch without emotion or care for any victim. At the war's end he possessed only one skill to exploit, becoming a killer for hire, a lucrative occupation it turned out as his reputation increased. He never met the clients. He was mailed his instructions and details on each victim, to protect his anonymity. He never asked why they were to be killed; he didn't care. What did he take from those years and ever since? Living your life with compassion or caring for others is an exploitable weakness. You do what you must do to survive in a godless world. Some of the eighty-two were just random strangers used to perfect his skills and satiate his anger.

There was a moral fork in the road, to the left regret and recrimination, to the right a moral landscape where life wasn't sacred. The contracts only had themselves to blame for the businesses they entered, the random killings were just in the wrong place at the wrong time, but thousands die every day for the same reason. The albums were black, leather bound and each with the same inscription on the inside page, from the Sufi mystic Rumi.

'When your heart becomes the grave of your secrets, '

Catherine Stewart glanced up as her secretary Jean put her head round the door.

'There's two detectives here to see you'.

Two familiar faces stood the other side of her glass wall.

'Tell them I've too much on today.'

Before the message could be relayed, Diana and Steph walked into the office. Diana sat down placing her large leather folder on the desk. 'We need to talk to you.'

Steph took the cue. 'We have more questions about your husband's death.'

'Jean, leave us.' Catherine turned to Diana. 'I thought we'd dealt with everything.'

Diana fiddled with her biro moving it around her fingers, then using it to make a point. 'We have current information to share. We now know Berwick's fall wasn't an accident, it was murder.'

A hand instinctively went to her mouth. 'Pardon?'

Steph carried on. 'We have completed the autopsy and it reveals he was murdered. Although falling from Sharp Edge might have caused his death, we found a fatal wound in his head caused by an object. With further tests we can identify the object and narrow down the possibilities. One item that does fit the profile is the ice pick that climbers carry with them. I am sorry to share this.'

Catherine's face drained of colour.

Diana took the moment to intervene. 'Mrs Stewart, can you think of anyone with a motive?'

'No! He was well liked. We have a settled life here; this doesn't make any sense at all.'

Diana's moment was ruined by the secretary entering, tray laden with drinks. All the time Catherine looked at Diana's blank face. Steph whispered a few words to the secretary before she went out the office door. Diana continued.

'Run through all your movements of the day again. You told us you drove Berwick to Threlkeld in the morning, left him to make his own way back. Correct?'

Catherine nodded. Diana carried on. 'I'm confused, tell me again why didn't you report him missing until the next day, weren't you worried?'

'Like I told you, I assumed he got drunk, stayed at the pub, he's done that before.'

'We have some new information. Do you know Peter Braithwaite?'

'Yes, he is a friend of ours, what's he got to do with this?'

Diana intertwined her fingers, putting her elbows on the desk. 'Mister Braithwaite tells us that you and Berwick were staying with him and his wife in a cottage in Threlkeld. He also told us that you and Berwick went off walking together that day.'

Catherine stood up, looking out the office window, then turned back.

'OK, It's true. We climbed up Blencathra that day. I haven't told you because what I told him that day was painful.' Catherine words were stuttered. 'I told him I'd been having an affair, he stormed off. I felt guilty. I thought in his torment he was reckless, that's why he fell. It was my error.'

Diana leapt in. 'You didn't follow him to take the opportunity to get him out of your life.'

For the first time Catherine showed real hurt staring across at Diana. 'Get a grip. You don't kill because of an affair, you either leave them or make up. What's my motive for killing him, that's ridiculous?'

'Do you own an ice pick?'

'No, I don't, I'm not a climber, only an occasional walker?'

'Did Berwick?'

The retort was sharp. 'No idea.'

Diana and Steph went silent, Catherine cracked. 'We did have a perfect marriage till the last two years. I told you before he has been obsessed with his endeavours, as he calls them. Another man came along who paid me welcome attention.'

Steph spoke. 'Who?'

'I'd rather not say.'

Diana stood up pointing with her pen. 'Mrs Stewart you have held back on key information, which makes you a suspect. For your information people have killed when having affairs. There's usually a hidden reason, money, envy, jealousy. I ask again who is the affair with?'

Catherine took a breath, 'Can this not get out yet. It's his boss Mark French at Sellafield. It's been going on a few months, yes, it is serious, I was going to try for a divorce, you can check with my solicitor. It may sound crass, but we are in love and are to be married. Berwick was a senior scientist, not a rich man. I was happy to not contest, he could keep everything, it's the least I could owe him.'

Steph smirked. 'Easy, now he's dead.'

'I told you. See my solicitor, he will confirm all this. For Mark's sake can this be confidential.

Diana asked. 'Your story is you left him on Blencathra, and he wandered off. How was he?'

'Furious, shouting, what do you think!'

'Did you see anyone?'

'No, I took the straightforward path down into Threlkeld. Drove to the cottage to collect my things, before driving home. When I got home, I rang Mark to tell him what happened, check my phone records. That alibi enough?'

Diana and Steph both stood up. Diana put her card on the desk. 'That's all. This isn't over, you haven't got an alibi. You could have followed him off the mountain, killed him on Sharp Edge, drove home to make that call. A warrant is coming this afternoon to search your home. Don't get ideas to go and remove any items, we have an Officer stationed outside. We clear?'

As Diana and Steph sped out of the car park, Catherine dialled a number on her phone, only to get voicemail, the message was brief. 'You need to call me.'

Five minutes down the road Diana turned to Steph. 'I think she's right. The motive is weak. Check the solicitor and her phone record. My intuition tells me it's not her.'

A few more minutes silence, Diana put on her music.

Steph was quizzical. 'Who's this?'

'Bruce Springsteen.'

'Not a fan.'

'People aren't, till they see him live, after that they are hooked. I've seen him ten times, some fans have been to hundreds of concerts. A Bruce concert is a carnival ride, they're never shorter than three hours.

Steph smiled. Her Boss sounded cheerful almost enthusiastic.

'Go on, convince me.'

Diana turned. 'You mean it?'

'Yes,'

'OK, here's my Bruce memory. The last tour I decided to see him in New York, a birthday treat. He played for four hours; it was brilliant. I booked to stay at the Plaza. I didn't realize that Bruce and the East Street Band were also staying. I ended up in the Oak Room bar with them consuming a lot of drinks after the gig. Bruce put one arm round my shoulder, the other cuddling a bottle of Bourbon. They got out their guitars, singing all sorts and I was joining in, being part of the East Street Band, the greatest rock 'n' roll band in the world.'

16

Slim Slow Slider

July 26th

Neil Denver sauntered from his office at MI5, across Parliament Square, three minutes later making it to Westminster Bridge. At six foot three, Neil peered above most commuters and tourists. His brown, gelled hair was neat and parted on one side, not a single strand out of place. He had his own uniform. A crisp white, Oxford, button down shirt, plain blue tie, a three-piece black, single-breasted suit, and black Churches' brogues. His bearing, his walk, and his dress hid his working-class origins in Battersea. They were all a product of the scholarship he won to Cambridge and his period of service in The Coldstream Guards, which enabled him to upgrade his accent, his appearance, and his manner. But he was a great believer that you can take the boy out of Battersea, but you can't take Battersea out of the boy.

Tonight, it was a blood-red sunset up the river towards Putney and the familiar smell of the Thames like a damp basement. The river was flowing slowly and he remembered the aged stories of the Thames when it was frozen. As it was thirty minutes before his train, he took the time to stand on the bridge to take it all in one last time. This would be his first time north again since the February bombing. A blot on his MI5 career.

He joined the melee down towards the London Eye. The embankment was crowded with sightseers, so he took the alternative route down York Road, walking faster when the first raindrops fell. His mobile rang, it was his junior.

'Sir, my view is that the security at Sellafield needs beefing up. I'm seeing French tomorrow morning if you can make it in time.'

'John, you're right, this has to be shutdown tight. It's already getting out of hand; you have full discretion. I'll try to get up soon, but I've got one last thing to sort out in London first.'

'Boss, by the way, we have a policewoman sniffing around. A DCI, Diana Petrou.'

'Leave her alone. We partnered before on the PM's security. She was a decent copper but got caught in that bombing in February afterwards a breakdown. I'll talk to her myself.'

James Randolph Maximillian Edward French, 73, retired Lieutenant General, former equerry to the Queen, Winchester educated, because nobody of class goes to Eton, poured himself another fine malt whisky. He rolled the Glencairn crystal glass between his palms before swallowing the precious Glenfiddich Grand in one gulp. The faintest sharp taste rested on the tongue to savour. He poured himself another. The phone rang.

'Hello Father, what are you doing?'

James dipped a finger, savouring the taste, annoyed at the interruption, from his son Mark.

'Enjoying a whisky, what are you calling about?'

Mark ignored the rebuff, typical of the lack of warmth he experienced all his life, so he bit back. 'Nice to chat to you too. I have to ask you about someone I met briefly at your retirement bash.'

'Might be difficult, I was out of it most of the night. I do remember the interminable speeches, strangers, your mother, as always, out of place. I thought it was all Army.'

Mark couldn't resist a dig. 'Yes, your batman Henry came with that ridiculous ice sculpture.'

James adopted his default superior tone, words like scissors cutting through paper. 'How dare you! That was a wonderful gift. It was an exquisite carved head of my favourite horse, High Hopes.'

'Yup the horse you cared for more than us. What a gift, it melted away the next day into a pool of water. Like you, nothing lasts.'

James took another shot of whisky. 'I won't apologise son, I served my country well, all those years in India, Kenya and Aden. I was a proud member of the Coldstream Guards, your mother, unlike you, supported me. She was a dutiful wife.'

Mark held back his temper. 'It wasn't only Army people at that do. I remember a lot of government suits. I have dealings with a man at the moment that I think you know, Neil Denver.'

The response was instant. 'Don't mess with him. He's senior MI5, ex-Coldstream too. He specialises in tidying up government messes, ruthless and charming. You remember the major corruption scandal two years ago at the Home Office?'

'No.'

'Exactly. Tread carefully boy, promise me you are not behaving in a stupid manner. MI5 operates as a hegemony. My advice son, avoid meetings alone, never accept an offer for a drink and don't dally words with him. Can I get back to my Glenfiddich? It's the last of my 55?'

'What's wrong with the Super? The door's locked and he's sat at his desk, staring into space.'

Steph looked at Martins. 'What?'

'It's the Super, he's been odd all day.'

'Maybe he's wondering how to sack you. Leave him alone.'

Superintendent Ingles looked at his shaking hands. He finally decided. He fumbled around for the burner phone from the bottom drawer and hit the only number in speed dial. At the tenth ring the answer switched to voice mail. Ingles turned around to face the back wall.

'Look, I've just seen the results from Berwick's autopsy, he was murdered. Is this your doing? I never signed up for this, just passing on info. As far as I'm concerned that's me...'

Before he could say the final word, the VM finished.

Two hours later, the dentist was explaining, 'Julian there's a couple of filings to do, I'll numb the gum and come back in five when it's worked. Let's lower the chair down.'

Ingles closed his eyes, breathing deeply, thinking, 'I'll call him again, arrange a meeting, tell him I don't want more money.'

The feel was of a ring of cold steel pressed against his forehead. About to shout, a man in a balaclava pressed a hand across his mouth and shook his head. He spoke with an accent Ingles couldn't recognise.

'Have you ever seen Marathon Man?'

The reply was wide eyes and shaking legs. The man reached across and picked out a drill with a single sharp point.

'I thought it was all a bit unrealistic. Keeping inflicting pain whilst asking, is it safe. He didn't need to do that to get an answer.'

The man was now sitting across Ingles chest pinning him to the table, the gun still forced against his forehead, the drill in the other hand. Words stuttered out from Ingles mouth. 'Wha, wha, what do you want?'

'I come bearing tidings from our mutual friend. He is displeased with your attitude and insistent that you carry on with your efforts on his behalf. But in case you are not convinced I have come to ensure you do.'

The drill switched on. 'You will do as you are told, or you will lose both eyes.'

Ingles screamed as the point of the drill came closer and closer to his left eye. The drill switched off as it touched his eyelid.

The dentist was banging on the locked door, 'Let me in!'

'Superintendent the next time I won't stop and after I've finished with you, I'll pay a visit to your wife. Nod if you understand.'

The man backed away, unlocked the door, shoved the dentist onto the floor and walked out.

'Di, where have you been, your phone was off.'

'I switched it off Steph, just wanted a little peace and quiet to think about all this.'

'More Bruce I suppose? There's good news and bad news.'

'Go on, tell me,'

'The Army rang. We have more info on John Castle. In Afghanistan they discerned what a crack shot he was and he was trained as a sniper. He went to a suspected Taliban meeting, tasked to take out the known leaders. It turned out that there were American soldiers there and a friendly fire incident happened, but they won't give any more details. After the incident he was discharged, sent for PTS therapy. Their opinion he never recovered from what he did.'

'The bad news?'

'This is really bad. There's another body. Old Gabriel Wood. He's sailed on Windermere for over 60 years, a real character in Ambleside, always in his yellow cagoul and battered sailing pumps. You might have seen him, distinctive bent nose from not ducking when the boom came across once. And get this, his body was washed up below Wray Castle. Like the others he was a regular sailor out on the Lake. Blackpool examined the body and thinks he'll confirm it in autopsy that there's a similar bullet wound in the head, so betting we have the same killer. We'll know more when he can examine the bullet.

'Did he have any links to Givens or Wilson?

'No immediate links that we know about. He's retired now. He used to run pleasures cruises. This is awful Di, he was really well liked, a character, a fixture, hard to find anyone who would have a reason to kill him. No family by the way, he never married.'

'On the face of it we have a serial killer, John Castle. But there's another possibility. Castle is a hired killer, hired to kill

Givens and Wilson and killing Gabriel is to make us keep thinking it's a serial killer.'

'Di, isn't that a stretch, a serial killer still makes more sense.'

'Agreed, but we desperately need to find Castle. If he is a serial killer, anyone else out on Windermere is at risk. We need more evidence, everything we have is still circumstantial. With Gabriel's death we need witnesses who may have seen where he was when he was shot and from what Blackpool said we might be able to better pinpoint where the shooter was.'

'Still a long shot. But ask Blackpool if he can do this from the three killings so far and put out an appeal for witnesses again on all three killings. And I don't care how long it takes I want searches of any CCTV.'

'I'll get Gabriel's place searched and talk to any friends just to double check there's no links to the other killings.'

17

Day is done.

July 27th

It was after seven when Steph stepped out of Windermere Police Station, turning around at the sound of her name. Twenty yards away Mel Wilson was waving at her with a large white envelope.

He walked up to her, speaking softly. 'Detective this is for you. I needed to go through all Dad's papers for Probate. I want to be truthful with you. I promise you; I was never ever involved with my Father's business or his death or Kim's.' Steph took the envelope as Mel turned and ran off.

There were five sheets of handwritten A4, recording shipments with dates, amounts and prices and all destined for Dan Jetty. At the bottom of the last page was a note addressed to Mel, from his father. It read, 'If anything happens to me, these are proof of my dealings with Jetty. Each order is for cannabis and cocaine smuggled in with our equipment. If I am killed, take this to the Police. I also know that Jetty threatened to kill Givens if she didn't have an abortion.'

The screes of Wastwater were turning a radiant purple in the twilight, mirrored on the water's darkening surface. Castle had been contemplating the changing hues of the screes for two hours on the opposite side of the lake. Wastwater, the deepest lake, with the steep slope on one side, enclosed in an arc of high fells, made it feel like the most mysterious and lonely place. He marched on, a mile, beyond the grey waters, to the tiny church of St Olaf. He read the names on the gravestones of families, all those fallen to their death on the fells above. In the cloudless dimming light, Great Gable stood towering above its neighbours. A profile like any youngster's drawing of what they thought a mountain was like, a pyramid with symmetrical sides. He had ascended it many times, but only from Wasdale. The last time he'd been at the summit was on November 11th, for the annual remembrance service.

He pulled the straps of his framed backpack tight and stepped forward. Great Gable was distinct from other fells. The path was visible all the way to the summit. To halfway, it was an effortless ascent on a wide path of bedded gravel. After that it turned to a scramble over rocks and boulders, searching for hand holds, before turning left to avoid the daunting rock faces of the Great Napes and Westmoreland Crags. At halfway, the sun had set. Two hours later, by torchlight, he reached the Summit.

Standing on top of the cairn, little was visible to the north, south or west and behind him Wastwater was like a black shadow, in the moonlight. He knew that to three sides it was rough, steep descents over slipping stones and partial vegetation but not a worry tonight. Great Gable, he thought, is a favourite fell but not the most superior. Lacking tarns, outcrops hiding views of what may lay ahead, and Sharp Edge, it couldn't match Blencathra.

He took a few steps down, sat, and rested against a rockface bearing the bronze memorial to the dead of world war one, erected in 1924. He slipped on his fleece, rummaged in his backpack, taking out his favourite meat pie from The Pie Shop in Ambleside. The perfect balance of pastry, choice beef, onion, gravy and for once he could savour each mouthful in silence without intrusive chatter from other walkers to disturb his enjoyment. He pressed one hand against the cold bronze in a precious ritual to read aloud all the names before drinking five toasts of Taliskers, for his fifth regiment comrades.

From his bag he took out a sealed envelope and pinned it to his jacket. The envelope was addressed, To Whom It May Concern, signed Corporal John Castle. He reached in the backpack, pulling out his Army Browning semi-automatic and placed the barrel in his mouth.

The peace was shattered by a loud banging on the door and a voice shouting for DC Giles. Steph slipped on a robe and called down the stairs. 'I'm coming.'

Steph opened the door, keeping it on the chain.

'DC Giles?'

'Yes.'

The man flashed a warrant card. 'I'm DC Viner, from the county drugs squad,'

'What are you doing here this time of night?'

Viner handed over a piece of paper, 'We have a warrant to search your house, let us in.'

'OK, let me get dressed first.'

'No, I insist you let us in otherwise we will break the door down.'

Steph noticed the two PCs, one carrying the battering iron. Steph slipped off the chain and three bodies pushed her aside.

'Heh, wait a minute, before you start tearing the place apart, courtesy for a fellow officer. What is this about?'

'We have received reliable information that you are in possession of cocaine, hence this warrant which allows us to search the whole premises, including your garden and your vehicle. Is anyone else here?'

Martine appeared at the top of the stairs in a nightdress.

'Martine, these are all police, they have a warrant to search the place, they claim we have drugs here, come down and put a coat on.'

Steph held out her hand for the warrant. 'Now DC Viner, who has told you this.'

'I am here under the instructions of DC Martins. If it's rubbish, we'll find nothing. We can't ignore information like this. I suggest you both sit on that settee to let us get on with this. How about some tea?'

'Get on with it.'

The two PCs disappeared upstairs. Viner started sorting through the shelves before shifting Steph and Martine off the settee. Viner threw the cushions onto the floor and searched down the sides, turned the settee on its back, shining a torch through the gauze support. Finding nothing he went off into the hallway, searching through the pockets of all the coats on the rack.

After another fifteen minutes the two PCs appeared downstairs. 'Nothing upstairs Sir.'

'Viner, is that it?'

'That leaves your car, can I have the keys and where is it?'

Step pointed at the hooks on the wall. Three policemen followed her into the street. She unlocked the Audi. They got to the boot last, pulled out the carpet, shining a torch, to reveal the spare and the tools. There it was, a white rectangular packet. Viner turned to Giles who said nothing. Using a penknife he slit the top to expose the inevitable white powder and tasted some on the tip of a finger.

'DC Giles, I am arresting you on suspicion of possessing a class A drug. You do not have to say anything. It may harm your defence if you do not mention, when questioned, something which you later rely on in court. Anything you do say may be given in evidence. I suggest we go inside and you get dressed.'

Steph, walking out, handcuffed, shouted out. 'Martine, ring Diana, tell her what's happened, they are taking me in and Martins has stitched me up.'

Part Two

Confession

If we confess our sins, he is faithful and just, to forgive us our sins and to cleanse us from all unrighteousness.
1 John 1:9

18

Candy's Room

July 27th

Drowsy, Diana fumbled for her phone beside her lounge light. A notification flashed of a message on her text. She tapped the app. What followed woke her in an instant. It was an animation of her kids being shot, taken outside her house, with a voice saying, 'Go home, don't come back.'

Hurtling down towards the M6, Diana hit the first number on her speed dial, on her hands free, reaching voice mail. 'Steph, it's Diana. I have to go back home, a problem with my youngest. I maybe away for a couple of days, can you tell Ingles. He won't be happy but family comes first. When I am away can you do some more digging. Up the effort to find John Castle, he could be our serial killer, or maybe hired by Jetty? After what Blackpool told us about Berwick Stewart, we've got two separate killers to chase. See what more you can find on this Berwick bloke and his wife, I'm sure she wasn't telling us all she knows. Poke around, did Adam Wilson have any links to Jetty, could we have drug related killings? One more thing…' At that point, the VM ran out. Diana cursed and thought she'd call again later.

An hour on, she was in her old guvnor's office. She showed the video and secured the promise of patrols outside the house and at the school. With her old force's capabilities, they tracked the source of the video, inevitably to a burner phone. She left them examining the video itself for any clues.

Midnight, she was settled on the settee next to her husband James, with a cappuccino in hand. Coming home to the City she called home, where she lived since she was ten years old, when the family relocated from Santorini. There was time to spend with Jane and Jack. Jane was changing fast, fourteen going on eighteen. Jack, twelve years of stubbornness, rejecting Rugby League that James played all his adult life, in favour of football. Typical of teenagers they were choosing not to go to Sunday school, beginning to reject the Christian faith that had been her rock, all her life. Thirty years in the City Police Force she'd seen all types of crime but, after February, she knew evil was a reality.

She thought about when she and James met, twenty years ago in Paris. She was drinking coffee on the Champs-Elysees, remonstrating in English with the waiter. After listening for a few minutes James decided to help her, trying to settle a dispute about an overcharge.

She was stunning in those days. Smiling blue eyes, pale skin hidden from the sun by her wide straw hat. She offered a handshake with thin, elegant fingers and introduced herself. 'I'm Diana.'

He perused the bill. 'I'm a regular here. I'm sorry to tell you that's the correct charge. You pay a premium for drinking on the Boulevard.'

'That's such a rip off. Can you tell him from me, I apologise for making such a fuss?'

'*Monsieur, La dame s'excuse. Je l'ai explique a elle.*'

The waiter made a snorting noise before disappearing inside. She offered a thank you drink at a cheaper cafe. At that point, the next twenty years started. He remained striking to the eye. James avoided the beer bellies of colleagues his age. Together they were determined to stay fit, with a daily run, a circuit at the gym, at least twice a week. The only sign of James aging was the greying dark hair.

James exclaimed, exasperated. 'Diana, you listening to me?'

'Sorry, miles away. What are you saying?'

'Look, you did the right thing telling me about the threat. We'll keep it from the kids and I've got the Superintendents' number to ring if we are worried about anything.'

'James, this is just trying to frighten me off. I don't think for a moment these people would be stupid enough to harm a copper's kids, but protection is all arranged. I know who's doing this and he's going to face the full force when I get back.'

'When are you setting off?

'In an hour.'

'I did think you being in the Lakes was for the best, till this. There's too many reminders in this city. We're near the stadium; you could be walking past it each day. You still aren't healed. The wounds are improving but it's what's going on inside I worry about.'

Diana swiped the chocolate from her cappuccino with her forefinger and licked it off.

'I've been angry, irritable, unforgiving. I'm regretful for what I have put you and the kids through. It's left me totally uncertain about myself at the moment. I go through a mental masochism each day.'

James hugged his wife. 'They are accurate in their diagnosis, it's PTSD you are suffering from, which isn't a surprise. Surviving whilst people died is not a reason to blame yourself, without you many more might have died.'

The tortured shame of the truth bit hard, the words froze. She could only nod. Her phone showed a notification of a voice mail. She pressed play. Martine's voice was tearful and frantic. Fists clenched; Diana thought, this must be Jetty and for Steph this could be the end of her career. It was the time to fix the bastard and Martins, she'd sort that bastard too.

July 28th

The Evidence room was primitive. Diana engaged one of the PCs in conversation, suggested he get her a coffee, picked up his security card from his desk and swiped in.

Facing her were four rows of steel racks, full of the same light brown, cardboard boxes, each with a label showing its case identification. Diana peered at her smartphone for the number she copied from the register. She found the box in the fourth rack and pulled it onto the floor. Two voices came into the room. She lifted the box back into its slot and waited anxiously. The chattering was discussing last night's football.

'I'll go down here; you try the last row.'

Diana got down on her haunches, peering at box labels as a PC came around the last metal row. 'Hi, can I help?'

Diana stayed where she was, face turned to the wall, not answering. The PC started to walk towards her when the other voice called out. 'I've found it, c'mon.'

With that the PC turned and walked away. Diana pulled down the box again, transferring a plastic bag into her coat pocket. She hunted for the other box, taking out a single item.

'I've been telling you two all along that it was a serial killer. Today, up on Great Gable, two walkers found Castle. He shot himself. It got to him finally. To me that's it ended. I'll get Blackpool to do an autopsy. I've sent Martins to go through his house for any material. You two can concentrate on Jetty for drug dealing. That man needs bringing down, his dealing is getting out of hand. Don't waste any more time trying to find links to the murders. Are we clear?'

Diana called out as Ingles walked away. 'Was there a suicide note?'

Ingles turned. 'They're sending it over.'

'How can we be certain he killed these three?'

Ingles shook his fist, shouting. 'I'm telling you, damn it; he's the killer. We will find the evidence. Go focus on Jetty. You keep forgetting who's in charge here.'

The torrent of abuse didn't abate. 'Castle fits the profile, psychologically damaged from what the Army asked of him, being detached from the kill, distant from the result. He gets satisfaction from the act, from the skill, from the killing not the kill. Givens, Wilson, and Gabriel were perfect targets on Lake Windermere. Alright!'

Back in his office, Ingles knew the problem was finding the proof, given that the wilds of the Lake District used minimal CCTV. His awful thought was, if Castle weren't the killer, only another murder would prove it, but he's an available scapegoat.

He sat at his desk and dialled a former public-school buddy at MI5.

The Church was a quaint converted house of Lakeland stone and wood. Diana's home church was huge, holding over 800 people. Here, twenty people filled this room. Without musicians, the hymns were sung acapella. They all knew the words of 'Be Thou My Vision.' A few notices followed; helping Jim with his house move plus a venue for a summer Barbecue. All gentle compared to the evangelical preaching at her city church, to help the homeless, to befriend nascent gangs. She wasn't listening to the sermon, when for some reason the Pastor's words broke through. 'Be on your guard, stand firm in the faith, be courageous, be strong' which seemed apt in the circumstances. Diana felt her feet were on shifting sands, having spent the day in rising anxiety from the threat to her family and Steph's arrest.

When the service ended, Diana approached the Pastor. After introductions and a few pleasantries, he took Diana to a corner, to sit on two wooden, collapsible chairs.

Diana struggled to start. 'Pastor, do you think I can be a Policewoman and a committed Christian?

Ray smiled, speaking whilst stroking his dark grey beard. He claimed, although being a police officer might bring more difficulties, other jobs brought similar challenges.

Diana's expression showed she heard all this before. She asked. 'Does God accept the ends justifying the means, to bring evil people to justice or to halt an evil?'

Ray replied, 'God doesn't have ends and means, he helps you live right today.'

Diana threw her hands wide in frustration. 'Rubbish, what a cop out!'

Silence followed.

'Diana tell me what you're thinking. Are you talking about something that happened to you?'

Diana stared at the floor. Silence descended again.

'If you can't tell me what happened, remember God is a forgiving God.'

Diana stayed silent, so Ray continued. 'Diana, Jesus is merciful but if you have done something that's troubling you remember what's written in 1 John 1:9. It says, *If we confess our sins, he is faithful and just and will forgive us our sins and purify us from all unrighteousness.*'

After a moment Diana spoke. 'In February I was at a terrorist bombing. Maybe you read about it. I shot a terrorist, but not before he set off his suicide vest and killed eight people and maimed others.'

'I do recognise you now and I remember the story. You received commendations for stopping him getting to the football terraces. Yes?'

'That's not the full story.'

' Can you tell me about it?'

'No, It's too painful. All I know is, I have to atone for what I did.'

Ray's last words followed Diana as she walked out of the room. 'Diana, atonement isn't down to you. Christ has atoned for you.'

Diana sat in the park. She'd been through this with the therapist they made her go to. But the shame from the bombing was still bottled up inside.

Walking helped, so she headed up the easy but steep climb to Wansfell summit. She had endured four visits to the assigned therapist, necessary to get signed off as fit to go back home. The therapist, of course, wanted to know about her childhood, so she laid out the expurgated version. She felt no love for her father just fear. A slap from her father's right-hand was delivered for the smallest infraction. Sitting, petrified, the father towering over like an unbending oak. The arc of terror swung, landing precisely on a left ear each time. The face that showed no emotion, no anger and a mother who would hide away in the kitchen. What did she learn from childhood? Never break the rules, have clean, shiny shoes, wash up any used plates. Have a tidy spotless bedroom, never spill the toothpaste, finish everything on the plate, shoes off before treading on the carpet, collecting up all the leaves in the garden. Father was convinced this was the best way to raise a child and prepare them for the world. Why? Because that's how he was raised.

The therapist asked. 'What happened?'

'I left home at sixteen and joined the police force, a place of rules and fighting injustice I naively thought. I think my father was disappointed with his life, never achieving anything significant. I've forgiven him but forgiving someone doesn't mean you forget. My life feels like a symptom of a past cancer.

Diana lied about the panic attacks, lied about the effect of the murders, lied about her memories, lied about her fits of anger, lied about the underlying causes of her breakdown. Challenged she rolled up her shirt sleeves and showed the scars, typically the therapist said she was here for the scars inside. The crunch came when she started to walk out, mumbling,

'This is bullshit.'

The therapist called out, 'Do you know how to destroy an iron bar? Just leave it in damp air and it will overtime eat itself away as it turns to rust. You saw eight people die. You are in a scene of darkness. In that darkness, that's where the treasures may lie, and the path back. If you run away, it will all get worse.'

Diana turned back. 'So here's the reality, I'm on a nowhere path with an unchangeable past and a handcuffed future, stuck in today's torment. And that's the truth.'

A crowd gathered at Wansfell's summit, delighting in the afternoon sunshine. Diana passed them by and found a spot with an undisturbed view out over Windermere and took several swigs from her water bottle. She recalled the moment at a summer camp when she was fifteen when she committed her life to Christ, not realising that it wasn't an easy choice to become a Christian. People who don't comprehend what it demands of you.

Being a police officer, the relentless criminal dealings she faced each day could breed cynicism. She was always in a state of ambiguity, always in a spiritual battle. She hung onto one thought in the darkest hours, that Christianity was the path where salvation didn't come from good deeds. It was instead from belief and faith an human failings and could be forgiven. She remembered once hearing that faith without doubt is like a human without antibodies. For such a time her faith was like a train going backwards in a tunnel receding from the light until that blinding moment and a Pastor, a therapist altered that. She knew why she was inflicted with a gnawing shame, like a silent killer working inside towards a tipping point. What could she do to atone? Will finding these killers do it?

19

Northern Sky

July 29th

The dust rose into grey transient clouds from each footstep as he walked across the floor of the deserted warehouse. Pulleys hanging from the ceiling were the only reminder of the boxes of tools, stacks of bricks and bags of cement once stored. He pulled up a chair and sat dead centre in the decaying room. He peeled and ate the orange segment by segment. Tearing the peel into smaller and smaller fragments was a sort of meditation to focus the mind.

The metal door creaked. Mel Wilson almost ran into the room, calling out, 'What's this about?'

The man pulled the Glock from his jacket pocket and shot, in one smooth movement. The bullet tore through Mel's chest, through the ribs and straight into his beating heart. Mel gasped, let out a final scream and collapsed to the floor like a stringless puppet. The bright red blood coalesced with the grey dirt turning it claret.

He walked over and shot two more bullets into the head and traced RIP with the tip of his trainers, into the spreading remnants of a life.

'Mel, just in case you had ideas to take over your father's side of the business. I now run the whole show.'

He covered the body in petrol and casually threw on a match as he walked away.

Ingles called Diana into his room. 'We have a dilemma. Last night, person or persons unknown broke into the evidence room, taking the opportunity to use a security card from one of the PCs, when he went to the canteen.'

'What did they take?'

'Two things. First, the cocaine found in Giles' car, second the knife found on Jetty when we arrested him and what a surprise neither went through forensics, which was due today. So we have no proof the cocaine belonged to Giles and it's easier for her to claim it was planted by Jetty. A car is easy to break into and it was easily found. The drug squad have admitted Martins took an anonymous telephone tip off. The arrest is withdrawn so Giles can return to duty. She must watch out though, the drug squad don't like failure.'

'We can't have one of ours fitted up.'

'I went through the building log for last night. You were in the building and one of the PCs reported someone, not uniform, was in the evidence room, but never saw enough to identify her, because it was a woman. A coincidence Petrou and your partner gets off the hook.'

Diana grinned. 'Pure coincidence'

'I'm convinced you did this but having one of ours charged won't do me or the force any favours. I guess you knew that too.'

Diana was still, staying impassive, until silence prompted a response. 'Well Super, Jetty gets off the hook too, why would I want that? I'm told it was Martins that took the anonymous tip off that gave the drug squad information on Giles.'

'And before you utter a word he acted in a proper manner.'

'If you say so.'

The confrontation with Martins was brief and sour. She cornered him in the gents and grabbed him by the throat.

'You bastard, your card's marked.'

Martins ended up on the floor hands shielding his head. She went to the custody sergeant to get Steph released.

Later, an agitated Steph was pushing at the office door, waving two envelopes.

'I hear the evidence went missing. Thanks.'

'No idea what you're talking about. Glad it's sorted.'

Steph grinned, passing over the first envelope. 'Mel Wilson stopped me yesterday and handed over this. There's sheets inside proving that Adam Wilson and Jetty were in business together. Wilson was smuggling Jetty's drugs inside his equipment orders from abroad. Wilson kept a private record in case anything happened to him.'

'Brilliant, well-done Steph. But is that a motive for having Wilson killed, unless Jetty has a new supplier? Get forensics on it, anything they can find. After what's happened to us both let's keep this just between you and me. We'll use when we have more on Jetty. What's in the other envelope?'

'Blackpool tells us that Castle was definitely a suicide. This was pinned to the body. A confession maybe.'

Ingles sat himself down at the front, the rest were on assorted chairs and desks.

Diana waited for silence. 'The information is that John Castle is dead. Committed suicide on Great Gable yesterday. This envelope was pinned to his coat and the fingerprints on it are his.'

Ingles interrupted. 'His confession, we have the serial killer.'

Diana scanned the handwritten contents of a single A4 folded sheet before reading it aloud.

'To Whom It May Concern.

I can't carry my burdens any longer. Being accused of something I did not do was the last straw. I came to Cumbria to live alone, to seek refuge in the Fells. I have not sought or desired friendship. I felt the best way to deal with my past was to be alone, to not inflict myself on anyone else. Why am I here? I was a sniper, drafted into the role without any mental assessment. Do you comprehend that shooting from a distance is both detached and personal? You choose the one individual; you shoot, he's dead, but you watch him before you shoot and you watch him die. Not the same as being in a battle where you're fighting for your own survival. A sniper kills without a threat to himself. I killed Taliban rebels in Afghanistan, convinced I was doing the right thing, until, like most of the soldiers I realised this wasn't the case. What were we fighting for? What were we achieving apart from watching good men die? One day I shot the wrong man. The official army document maintained it was a friendly fire incident. I shot an American Soldier by mistake, was dishonourably discharged, and evaluated to be a damaged person. What never came out was that I shot the GI deliberately. He was about to kill a Taliban he'd captured, in front of him. He shot first, I shot him. Ironically, I'd been positioned to provide defence for him and his unit. After that the nightmares began.

I've seen too much horror, too much degradation, too much hatred to believe in a God. If God existed, he'd wipe it all this away and start again. Humans kill each other, destroy the planet. Any decent qualities are always overridden by rapaciousness and self-preservation. Humans aren't worthy of any salvation. My nightmares have never gone away. I went to the Gun Club to release my frustrations but never killed anyone since leaving the Army. Believe me, I couldn't add to my nightmares. I killed for Queen and Country, never for myself. Ending my life is not an admission of guilt, it's at last to have a little peace. John Castle.'

'Few suicide notes where a person perversely lies. He's not our man.'

Ingles stood face to face with Diana. 'Petrou, come with me.'

The door was slammed shut. Ingles held the confession with an outstretched hand.

'You will lose this.'

'Pardon?'

'Castle is our man, and this just muddies the water. A loner, a sniper, and the killings have halted after Gabriel. I'm telling you; this is rubbish. Lose it and we hold a press conference announcing the killer.'

Diana stared hard at Ingles and then shook a finger at him.

'No, I won't. I've never lost or concocted evidence and I'm not about to start and worse it's obvious he's not the killer, so why are you so keen to not find the real killer?'

Ingles retaliated.

'Don't insult me, I'm your senior officer and I'm giving you an order. I'm covering up for nobody, this man is the killer and this,' waving the letter at Diana, 'piece of fiction is his last joke on us. I guarantee that's the end. We won't waste valuable time hunting for another culprit and you for once will follow an order.'

Diana took the letter from Ingles hand.

'I'm leaving this in a safe place and giving a copy to the team and we will persevere in hunting for the real killer.'

The shouted words, you're making a huge mistake, resonated as she slammed shut the office door. She knew the game in play.

Having finished another microwaved dinner, Diana relaxed with a cup of coffee, listening to Joni Mitchell. Her thoughts were subdued until the phone rang. She reached behind and knocked the receiver onto the floor. The effort to pick it up was annoying. The voice seemed familiar.

'Hello Diana.'

'Who is this?'

'I'm insulted that you don't remember me after all I did for you. It's Neil Denver. I thought I'd catch up; see how you are after the bombing, and how you are recovering in the Lakes; trust it's all going well.'

Diana sat up. 'Haven't heard from you since the bombing. You back in MI5?'

'Yes, back in the service. I heard they sent you to the Lakes.'

'You thought you'd catch up with an evening call. What are you after? C'mon, remember I know you well.'

'You thought you did. I have some questions for you about Berwick Stewart. I presume you have been told he was a senior scientist, based in a sensitive area at Sellafield on secret matters. I wondered what you have found out about his death. I'm given to understand it was an accident. Is that right?'

Diana's initial chuckle turned into a louder laugh. 'Here we go again. I don't believe a word of what you say. You are fishing for another purpose. In case you were going to offer, your help isn't required; we can find out on our own. Anyroad, isn't a call by you this late deliberate to catch me off guard?'

An unexpected question followed. 'Are you a Star Wars fan? I could quote Darth Vader. I find your lack of faith disturbing. I'm trying to help.'

'Darth Vader from the dark side, how appropriate, I promise I will keep MI5 informed of any significant developments but let's do it at a reasonable hour. I have a question for you. Have you come across Mark French?'

'I've never met him.'

'You are asking about Berwick Stewart, and French was his boss, but you've never met him. Interesting.'

'I've never met either of them. French has a senior role at Sellafield. I know he's ex-army, father is a retired Lieutenant Colonel from the Coldstream guards. I think he served in Bosnia and got a medal for saving locals. He's leading the decommissioning of part of the site. Why do you ask?'

'His PA Kim Givens was murdered. To quote Oscar Wilde, to lose one employee is a misfortune but to lose two isn't carelessness, more like suspicious.'

'It's a coincidence, I'm sure.'

Diana broke the ominous silence.

'How about this. My family was threatened to make me recuse from this case. I have that warning, and out of the blue you call me. Perhaps it's you guys recusing me from the case?'

Another silence.

'Nothing? One thing you can do for me. We have a suicide here of an ex-Army sniper, John Castle. Allegedly let go because of a friendly fire incident. Knowing the Army, that's not going to be the whole story. Can you check it out, bit of quid pro quo.'

'Let me see what I can unearth.'

Diana put the phone down and dialled another number, getting voice mail.

'Faria, It's DCI Petrou, can you call me in the morning when you pick this up.'

Diana needed another brandy and turned the music of 'Hissing of Summer Lawns' up loud. She remembered the first time she met Neil Denver. Minding her own business drinking in her favourite bar, Neil sat down next to her, introduced himself and started to talk. That was the first she heard about a potential bombing and that the chatter picked up online was that the PM could be the target. Turned out he was seconded from MI5 to head the PM's security detail. He was suggesting coordinating on security. At that point she was impressed with Neil and it didn't occur to her he wasn't being straight.

Now Diana knew Castle wasn't the killer, this was the right time to confront Dan Jetty. The all-black Range Rover, with tinted windows, turned onto the A591. Was this the drug dealer's car of choice? Diana kept her distance in the drive up from Ambleside to Keswick, made easier by it being still light after 9:30 in the lakes in July. Jetty headed for the central car park. Diana parked a few rows away and followed Jetty into the town. In the Public Bar of 'The Castle Inn', she ordered a tonic water and stood on her own in a corner, seeming to make a call. Seeing Jetty in person for the first time was unexpected. Over six-foot-tall maybe, in an ivory shirt, dark trousers and tasselled loafers, manicured hands, wearing a Rolex and a conventional short back and sides. The image was a smartly dressed businessman, the thug well hidden.

Diana observed several young men and women coming over to engage him in what seemed polite conversation. All his dealers perhaps. The men all exchanged handshakes; the women kissed him on each cheek. Diana waited until he was alone again, ordered two bottles of lager and passed one over.

'We haven't been introduced, I'm DCI Diana Petrou.

Jetty turned, smirking, 'Thanks for the drink. I've found out who you are. The big city copper who must have done something wrong to be sent here. I'm Dan Jetty, pleased to make your acquaintance.'

Diana gripped Jetty's right wrist tight and pulled him until they were locked together. 'Never, ever, threaten my family. Never ever go after my DC. Because you have, I'm going to shut you down, I'm going to get the proof you killed Kim Givens and Adam Wilson. I'm going to put you away.'

Jetty lifted Diana's hand from his wrist and held it tight. 'These are serious charges officer. I'm an honest businessman in import and export,' letting go he pointed behind him, 'I'm the employer of these fine men and women standing behind, who are keen to make your acquaintance.'

Diana felt an unaccustomed reckless anger and jabbed her fingers into Jetty's chest. 'You've been warned. Tomorrow, nine AM, Windermere police station, I have several questions. Don't be late.'

She was at the exit, before Jetty called out. 'You haven't finished your drink.'

Diana walked back, took the bottle from Jetty, downed it, and slammed it down on the bar. 'Don't be late.'

20

Climbing up the walls.

July 30th

Waking, Diana first saw a wooden cabinet supported by fluted columns, a chair like a wheelbarrow and silver light streaming through terracotta blinds. She strained to focus and felt exhausted with no clue where she was, and shivering, as some memories began to return.

She realised she was still in the clothes from last night and clambered out of the bed, sitting on its end. Staring at the wooden floorboards she tried to remember. The pub and threatening Jetty, leaving, walking to the car. She phoned Steph and left a message. Sitting in the car about to start the engine, suddenly disorientated, the lights around the car started to swirl and what then? A frightening feeling of losing control. She got out of the car, looking around the streetlights made fluorescent streams across a black starry sky. Whatever was happening was speeding up and she couldn't stop it. She tried closing her eyes, breathing deeply but all the world around was moving. Normality disappeared and her mind was in an escalating rush, like a flywheel gaining momentum on an unstoppable ride.

Later, after the initial panic, every car around her was changing colour, the tarmac glistening and the whole town was in motion. She tried to phone but the keys on her phone were dissolving. She walked back into the centre of the town towards the pub. The streetlight spotlighted faces all with strange expressions. Wandering the streets, it was like being in a dancing visual poem, gardens full of bright pansies, pink petunias and a pavement seemed to carry her forward, but still sweating with panic. The town became a nameless, startling place. Was it minutes or hours later that it morphed into darkness? She entered a stone building and immediately a mouth drying genuine fear rose and it felt like she was in an asylum, a situation she couldn't escape. She ran, slammed a door behind her and went down a spiral, cascading staircase to a stained marble floor. She stood on it and the floor liquidised, dragging her into a watery coffin, feeling powerless and paralysed.

She was shaking, sweating in that memory, when interrupted by a shout and a knock on a door. 'You awake?'

It took an effort to muster a reply before recognising that it was Steph's voice. 'Come in, where am I?'

Steph was dressed out of character in a long, silk kimono, her locks loose, not in the familiar bun. She smiled at Diana. 'Morning brought you a cup of coffee. You're in my house in Ambleside.'

'How did I get here?'

'Fiona, Sergeant Collins found you on a bench in the park, mumbling to yourself and called me. I thought it best to bring you back to my flat for some TLC. You were saying stuff that didn't make sense, till you fell asleep.'

Another voice was calling up. 'Is she OK?'

'She's fine, you go on, I'll catch you up later.'

A door slammed.

'Who's that?'

'My housemate Martine. Di, what did you take last night?'

'Nothing. I guess my drink was spiked when I was in The Castle Inn having words with Jetty. I've never taken drugs of any sort. What the hell was it?'

'Tell me what you remember.'

Diana paused before recounting fragments from the last hours. The chaotic visions, the fear, like fingers clinging on to reality's rock face.

'Di, what you've described, sounds like someone slipped Acid into your drink. You are welcome to stay here today to rest and get over it. I'm off to the nick, but I'll stay if you want me to.'

'No, just find out where Jetty is today. I'll be OK. This was his doing, trying to warn me off and trying to mess with my head.'

'Take care, we can't do without you.'

.

Hours later, eating a bowl of Steph's Arrabbiata, drinking a glass of Shiraz, the terrors subsided. They both collapsed onto the ageing sofa.

'Any update on Jetty.'

'He's disappeared, gone to ground. We've put out an APB.'

'So we now know he's prepared to take us on. First fitting you up and now this. Does that make him a killer too?

Diana suddenly noticed the music playing in the background. 'What's this annoying noise?'

'Radiohead.'

Diana averted her forward gaze and attempted a stare of derision at Steph. She punched her arm in play. Steph punched her back and laughed.

'Steph, what happened to a decent tune? Makes my tinnitus worse.'

'How awful is it?'

'Awful enough, a constant noise in my head like a boiling kettle. It first starts as hissing steam, or like air escaping from a tyre or like a dozen people at the same time going sssh. It's another aftermath of the bombing. I'm told it might go away, might get worse, depends on me. Avoiding Radiohead might be a perfect start. Downside, I can't wear headphones anymore or play the Stones full blast. I notice it when it's quiet. Strange it didn't seem to be there at all last night. It's unseen unlike the scars. If I seem like I am ignoring you, this might be why, or I choose to ignore you! Don't tell anyone else. I told you about my injuries before but never showed you.'

Diana stood and took off her shirt.

'I never realised.'

'Now they look worse than they feel.'

All down Diana's right side from her belt to her neck to either side onto her back and chest where what seemed hundreds of tiny white scars leaving little of her pink skin showing through.

'It's the same all down my right leg. When the bomb went off, I fell onto my side, protected my head with my right arm. The smithereens sliced through my shirt, my trousers, before I saved my face, blood was pouring everywhere. They shot me full of morphine. I stayed out of it for days. First months were painful, dressing changes. The scabs came off leaving all these scars. I'm all pink and white paisley. Perfect on the other side!'

Diana put her shirt back on. 'Thanks for today Steph and thanks to Martine. Let's meet up tomorrow at 9:00, see what we can do about Jetty. That bastard will pay. Why the hell do people take that drug for fun.'

At the door she turned with a smile. 'As the Queen Mother used to sign off, tinkety tonk and down with the Nazis, or in our case the nasties. Sleep well.'

21

Idiot wind

July 30th

Anti-corruption always started in a relaxed manner, handshakes all around.

'I'm DCI Geoff Painter; this is my colleague DC Brian Snape. DCI Petrou do sit down. Can I call you Diana?'

'If you must. How can I help you?'

'It's a pleasure to meet you by the way. You attended the Stadium bombing in February, yes?'

Diana snapped back. 'No. I didn't attend. I chased the bloody suspect through the City Centre and shot him before he could enter the terraces.'

Painter held up his hands. Snape sat still, notebook and pen in front of him on the desk.

'I apologise, I didn't want to make light of your heroics. The bomb going off caused repercussions for you?'

Diana laughed out loud. 'Nothing, part from damaged hearing and a body full of glass smithereens.'

'No, the breakdown you suffered afterwards. That's why you are here in the Lake District. Yes?'

Diana shifted downwards in her chair, extending her legs, waiting for them to get to the point. She smirked. 'No, I like the scenery.'

Painter feigned to read a report. 'It wasn't a choice to come, was it? I have a reliable source saying that you are having flashbacks, panic attacks and bouts of anger, which haven't gone away.'

Diana thought, OK we are getting closer to what they want, time to shut up.

Painter attempted to adopt a more official pose. 'Diana, this session is being recorded. I have witnesses telling me that these attacks are real. You have tried to conceal them from your colleagues.'

'It's debatable whether the source is reliable. Who is spreading these lies?'

'I have no obligation to reveal my sources at this stage. Be aware they are reliable.'

Diana tried her first strategy to gauge the reaction.

'Well, sod this for a fit up, I'm leaving.'

The placid voice became a loud, exclaimed command as Diana vacated her chair. 'DCI Petrou sit down! You walk out, and you can consider yourself suspended.'

At the door, Diana squeezed the handle hard, waited a few calculated moments before she turned back and sat down, smiling, thinking, that's quickened things up.

'OK, what else do you want to know?'

Painter turned over several papers on the desk. 'Are you on medication?'

'It's in the record, in front of you, citalopram for depression.'

Painter shut the folder. 'Diana, isn't it true that you are on other drugs too, illegal ones?'

At last, the cards were on the table.

'No, I am a serving police officer. I have never taken an illegal drug throughout my career, have never failed a drugs test. OK, this is what this shadow show is all about, another reliable witness, perhaps? What am I being fitted up for?'

'Were you not found in the early hours by your Sergeant after taking a class A drug?'

'No, I was rescued by Sergeant Collins after someone spiked my drink in a pub in Keswick.'

'So, you say. We have been informed that you went to that pub to buy cocaine and LSD.'

Diana couldn't help laughing. 'Tell me that's a believable scenario. I repeat, I am clean. I went to there to confront a Dan

111

Jetty. He is a known drug dealer and I believe involved with threats against my DC.'

'Isn't it the truth that you went to buy drugs and when he refused you assaulted him?'

Full hand displayed. They are so predictable. Painter tapped his pen on the desk. Diana, annoyed, gripped his fingers. Painter pulled away and carried on.

'Mr Jetty has made a formal complaint. We are obliged to investigate its validity and whether action should be taken. He claims on the night of the 30th around 10:00 PM, you assaulted him in The Castle Inn after he refused to sell you drugs that you were demanding. That you punched him in the stomach when he fell to the floor and you kicked him in the head and body several times. He is in Ambleside Cottage Hospital being treated. Where were you at 10:00 that night?'

Diana relaxed into the back of the chair, stretching out her legs again.

'I did not assault Mr Jetty. I asked him to come today for an interview, left and then found my drink was spiked and had a horrendous night. You have my word, which, from experience, is never enough for you bastards, who presume guilt before innocence, trying for another copper to make your quota for the year.'

'DCI Petrou, we are trying to get to the truth, Mr Jetty does have witnesses.'

'Oh, it's not Diana anymore!'

She stared back and took the moment to attack. 'Gentlemen, let me paint you the whole picture. Mr Jetty is first, aiming to extricate himself from a pending charge on supplying drugs. Secondly, he is implicated in three murders, his girlfriend, Kim Givens, his partner in crime Adam Wilson and Gabriel Wood. He also has found out that we are leaning on him to tells us about his suppliers. This is his pathetic way to discredit me, which he expects will get me off the case. You two you are doing his job for him. It'll take less than half a day with these dodgy witnesses to show this for the nonsense it is. You idiots have stumbled around, dragged me in without the most rudimentary investigation. What did you think? Bring down the City detective, make a name for yourselves?

For the first time Snape intervened. 'He says that you were drunk, do you have a drink problem?'

'No, I cope fine, thank you. You DC Snape, will address me by my rank and speak when you are spoken to. I came here to recuperate, an easy assignment but we have two murders. I am still a DCI and will do my job to find the murderer. If that includes upsetting our local low life, so be it. In case you don't know, that's our job. I won't tolerate a cover up. I refuse to answer any more questions until I have my Federation Rep with me. You, by the way, have extended your brief by not warning me that I could be charged with a crime and not allowing me to have my rep from the beginning. Therefore, what I have revealed up to this point is inadmissible. You have taped this session. Make a copy for me and if you don't supply it, I will instruct my rep to bring procedures against both of you under PACE. A Policewoman for twenty-five years I am familiar with how all this should go down. Let me tell you what you thought. You thought you would recommend to Ingles that I am restricted to desk duties and direct me not to go anywhere near Mr Jetty or his witnesses. Good luck with that. I suggest you get ready for the questions coming your way.'

Diana slammed the door behind her. Ingles barred her way into the squad room. Diana heard the usual from him, alter her attitude, this is serious, career could be finished, don't take Giles down too, don't go near Jetty, focus on the serial killer.

She shoved Ingles aside, found Steph and together they headed for a coffee.

Five minutes later they left Windermere nick, walking to the town through an unlit alley. Deep in conversation, Diana dropped the keys in her hand. Steph strode on ahead as Diana bent down to pick them up. She never heard the footsteps coming from behind.

A man grabbed Diana's hair, pulled her head back and pressed a knife against her throat. The accent was local. He spoke quietly. 'This is your last warning, get off this case, go home. That goes for her too.'

He threw Diana to the floor and ran back down the alley. By the time she stood and turned he was gone.

22

Us & them

July 31st

The room was a challenging murmur of National and Cumbrian journalists. Diana stood in the wings wiping sweaty hands on her trousers. Camera flashlights ignited as she stepped forward on to the stage. She couldn't afford a repetition of last time. She took her seat as Ingles stood.

'Thank you all for coming. This is an update on the investigation into the murders of Kim Givens, Adam Wilson and Gabriel Wood. DCI Petrou will read a prepared statement on the facts we have unearthed at this time and will take questions.'

Adjusting her denim jacket, Diana took a sharp breath and stepped forward. The silence of the room unnerved her as she started to speak. A voice at the back called out. 'Speak up, can't hear you.'

'Thank you for coming. I am DCI Petrou, lead investigator on these murders. Kim Givens, aged 24, was a personal assistant at Sellafield. She was single, a regular sailor on Lake Windermere each morning. Her body was found, washed up on the east shore of Windermere on the morning of July 17th. An autopsy revealed the cause of her death was from a single bullet wound entering through the back of her head. Adam Wilson, aged 48, was the owner of a construction firm, was married with one son Mel and a daughter, Isabel. Adam's body was found washed up on the west shore of the Lake, near Wray Castle, on the afternoon of July 20th. He was sailing that morning and was killed in a similar manner to Miss Givens, with a bullet through the back of his head. Gabriel Wood was a well-known character locally and an experienced sailor. In his seventies, retired, with no apparent connection at all to Wilson or Givens but was killed in a similar manner. I will take questions.'

The silence of the room erupted into a flurry of raised hands and shouts. Diana pointed to the nearest man in the front row.

'Are you saying another man was in the boats of these three people?'

'No, the autopsy reveals that by the nature of the entry wound and type of bullet, that both were shot from a distance. From the force of the shot they fell into the lake.'

The noise level rose again before she could point to a woman she recognised, from the Ambleside Herald. 'Shot from a distance, which takes real skill, like a sniper. Do you think we may have a serial killer?'

Ingles agitated, shouted above the cacophony. 'That is one possibility.'

Any semblance of order fell apart with shouts and screams. The woman shouted out.

'It sounds like a serial killer; shouldn't people be warned?'

Accusations flew around until Giles stood up, blew on her police whistle and the room quietened.

Ingles spoke again. 'Thank you, detective. I will conclude this unless we can conduct this press conference in a respectful manner. DCI Petrou, please explain where we have got to.'

'It is true that these killings take skill. Let's not jump to conclusions without corroboration. We are carrying out investigations into relevant places to identify anybody with the necessary skills to carry this out. However, we are investigating why these three particular people have been killed and if they have any links. It is possible that they are linked and killing them in this manner may have been decided by the fact that they were all known to be on the lake at particular times each day. There's a lack currently of any forensic evidence except the bullets, which have no fingerprints.'

The woman from the Herald rose again. 'You have an APB out on a Mr John Castle, could he be the killer?'

Diana waited for the clamour to die down. 'Mr Castle was found Sunday on Great Gable and had shot himself. The evidence we have indicates he was not the killer. His reasons for suicide were mental issues he was suffering, from his Army Service. Remember, the incidents in this country of serial killers are rare, so much so that we are familiar with the names of the towns, like Hungerford and Dunblane where they happened. I would conjecture that this is a wilful killing of three people. We haven't yet found the link. It's only speculation that this is a serial killer.'

'I'm Norman Button from the Lancaster Gazette. DCI Petrou, why are you here? Aren't you the detective involved in the terrorist bombing at the football stadium in February?'

Before Diana could respond, Ingles grabbed her arm. 'DCI Petrou is here to share her expertise with our force. That is all. We will hold a further press conference when we have more information to share, thank you.'

The woman from the Ambleside Herald shouted out.

'I've received a text that DC Giles was arrested under suspicion of drug dealing along with a Martine Clarke, have you any comment?'

At the door Ingles said thank you, leaving with a barrage of shouted questions.

Back in his office Ingles leaned on his desk with two clenched fists, shouting out.

'I'll find the bloody leak.'

Fiona Collins followed Ingles beckoning finger into the office and felt uneasy taking a seat. Ingles paced around the room, until he stood alongside her. 'How long have you been here?'

'Coming up twenty years now. I joined when I was eighteen, and never worked anywhere else.'

Ingles turned peering out of the window.

'I think we have the killer, this John Castle. The suicide note could be his last trick so he never gets remembered as a serial killer. Fiona, he fits the profile, expert shot, loaner, invalided out of the Army. I think DCI Petrou is not following my orders and without my knowledge is pursuing alternatives. The thought that Jetty is behind this is ridiculous. You know him Fiona, he strike you to be a man to do this?'

Collins looked over her shoulder. 'How would I know Super? Doesn't Castle's suicide note show he wasn't the killer. Jetty's business has got bigger, and we haven't gathered sufficient enough to nail him, yet.'

Ingles retorted. 'Collins, I want a daily report from you on the movements of the DCI and DC. You will inform me in person about anyone they are talking to, interviewing, or researching. I won't have a rogue operation in my station. We clear?'

'Sir, I am not comfortable with that, it puts me in a difficult position.'

The man bearing down on her was imposing and threatening.

'I, not anyone else, runs this place. You will follow my orders and I can further or ruin your career. You will see me each day for updates.' He stood back. 'Are they talking to anyone at Sellafield.'

'Yes Sir, about the man who died on Sharp Edge.'

'OK. Now get out.'

Looking up it was Diana's favourite barista. 'Hi Hazel, what brings you to the pub time forgot? I'm the bleary eyed one you see in the morning, always the same drink. Small skinny cappuccino. Did you know I'm a DCI?'

Hazel Day sat next to her. 'A policewoman, I didn't guess that, pegged you for a teacher.'

'You want a drink?'

'That's kind, I'll have G&T. What brings you to my favourite pub?'

Diana grinned at her and ordered two drinks. 'I'm hoping to catch Dan Jetty for a little chat. You come across him?'

'We all know Jetty and what he does. Drugs are not my thing. He is a bad sort. I was at school with him and he was a bully.'

Hazel took a large gulp of the G&T.

Diana stayed silent a moment, 'Maybe you can help me. I'm trying to track down Cody Beck. She's disappeared. Can you help with her?'

'I know who she is. She was a year above me at school. She was a bully and hung out with Jetty even then. I don't mix with those people, not my scene at all. What should I call you?'

Before Diana could answer, a familiar voice called behind.

'Hello Ma'am.'

It was DC Martins.

'You been interviewing my girlfriend.'

Diana turned to Hazel smiling. 'Despite what you said, you do keep dubious company.'

'Oh him, definitely. And now I know you're his boss, he could be in real trouble. If I hear owt about Jetty and Cody I'll tell Tim. Been a pleasure meeting you and thanks for the drink.'

Diana watched them wandering off hand in hand, thinking, she would still deal with Martins.

Propping up the bar were two Cumbrians chatting in a different language to Diana's ears. Was she a fish out of water here? She ordered another brandy. Three more appeared in the following hour, until Steph interrupted. 'How are you doin'?'

'Old, grumpy, difficult, self-pitying. More Brandy? I'm on my fifth or is it sixth?'

Giles shook her head and sat on the stool next to her.

'Wansfell Arms your local? Hope you're not driving.'

Diana ignored the comment. 'Cheers, what's brought you here?'

'Well, we have this wonderful, dilapidated pub of course which suits you. You seem to be trying to perfect the drunken detective role. Can't believe I'm saying this. I was worried about you. Barman Fred called me, thought you needed company.'

'Sod you Fred, next time mind your own business otherwise I will take my delightful company elsewhere,' Wagging a finger of censure, 'You are added to my pet hates list; spiders, John Humphreys and anywhere south of Stoke. If you get me another. You can join the pet likes; Spaniels, Charlie on Breakfast TV, and anywhere north of Stoke. Oh, and it may surprise you I do love cricket but can't fathom why England can't win at the Gabba.'

In the lunge forward to the bar for the brandy Diana spilled it on Steph's lap.

'Fred get me another and one for your snitch. Do you know, Ingles is like all the other men I have worked with, even the friendly ones, reluctant to trust my judgement. Always looking for affirmation from someone else. See, it might have appeared to change, that there's less prejudice, but now it's more covert than overt. Don't you think.'

'I trust your judgement but now you're talking gibberish about cricket I think it's time we left. I guess all this is because they gave you a grilling this morning in IA.'

Diana was about to speak. Steph placed a single finger on her lips.

Time and strong coffees brought Diana a modicum of coherence, relaxing in Steph's lounge.

'Steph I can feel it in my bones. This was all Jetty's doing, he's not the insignificant low life we thought. He tries to have you arrested, he spikes my drink and now has some thugs threaten my life. He's hired a killer to do the shootings and he is sitting on a quarter of a million in a hidden account. Maybe he killed Wilson because he knew too much, but again why kill the girl? But it is the same killer. She must have found something in his flat or overheard an incriminating conversation. Adam Wilson, I am sure is the supply chain. I bet drugs are brought in hidden in his business shipments. There's one reason to kill him, if Jetty has a more profitable supply chain, therefore, get rid of the person who could rat on him in revenge. Is he the only one bringing drugs in? Jetty must have other suppliers. My contacts know that drugs coming into cities in the North are from Cumbria. Why did Jetty go to Dublin days before the murders? Was that about organising a fresh supply route? So, all these pieces are in motion. I don't yet get the pattern. I'm drowning in theories. What's that word when there's no harmony? Dissonance, that's it, I'm drowning in dissonance.'

Steph sat silent until in exasperation, 'Di, take a breath. It's like you are on speed, slow down. We can talk again to Givens' mother. By the way Mel Wilson, no-one has seen him for days. His sister Isabel contacted us to report him missing. Maybe he's in hiding, doesn't want to talk to us or worse he's another victim. All of what you say maybe right, but it's supposition without real proof. You are flip-flopping between serial killer and Dan Jetty hiring a sniper.'

'Steph, I know you're right. Too many theories and not enough proof. What are we doing about Mel Wilson?'

'Collins is on the case. Looking at phone records and going through his office. It does look suspicious. There's no disturbance at his office, no communication with his sister or anyone else, except a call he took on the last day anyone saw him at his office. Looks like the call was from a burner.'

'This has to be linked to his father's killing. Was he involved with his Dad on something dodgy? Could it be the sniper, another shooting on the Lake and no body washed up yet?'

'Except, he wasn't a sailor. He never went out according to Isabel.'

Diana folded her arms. 'I've woken up to the fact I've tried living my life in the middle, and this is the result, I've been behind the curve. I'm done with that, it's like finding yourself in another's skin.

Steph laughed. 'Exactly what does that all mean?'

'Let's try a little danger, let's rattle the cages. First, we bring Jetty in. We can always find drugs to hold him. Could he be behind the Wilson murders, were they tied up in his dealings? They ran the perfect business to bring in drugs. Let's bring a few of the others in for questioning, make a show of it. Interview his mother, known dealers. Get him tailed all day, put the frighteners on the frequent customers. Let the press have the story we are concerned about drugs in Cumbria. Hint that it all maybe connected and see how he copes. We've been too light footed. I suppose Ingles will object. Get Martins to go through all Adam Wilson's business contacts and his accounts. By the way, Martins is in my bad books for what he did to you. Yup. It's about time we put the frighteners on. We haven't yet spoken to Kim's colleagues at Sellafield, to see what they can tell us. I'll make a call.'

'If that's Faria, can you trust her?'

Diana shrugged, dialled, a voice with clipped English and a German inflection answered.

'Hi, it's Faria, how can I help?'

'There's people at Sellafield who were friends with Kim Givens I need to see if they can shed any light on why she's been murdered. Can you set that up for me?'

'Of course, when should I arrange it?'

'Tomorrow if that's alright.'

'That's fine I've get you an office to use.'

Steph was drumming her fingers on a table. 'I'll come with you, but don't trust that woman. OK?'

'I know.'

'I'm going to speak out of turn, but I hope you will think it well meant. Drowning your sorrows is no answer. The brandy doesn't help your fitness or your mood. Di, it's not a solution.'

Steph waited for the rebuke, but it never came. Diana smiled and nodded her head.

23

Andmoreagain

August 1st

Steph chewed on an apple as Diana wound round the hairpins, ascending Hardknott Pass. For once it was an azure, blue sky day. The rising soft summer sun behind was making changing shadows on the road. At the summit, a beautiful view emerged of Wasdale to the North, Morecambe to the South and in the far distance, a tiny fragment on the sea, the Isle of Man. Steph spoke.

'Can I ask something. Are you OK? You don't seem the same ever since coming back.'

Diana took a few intakes of breath. 'This is between you and me, I don't need to be gossip fodder. Alright?'

'Of course Di.'

'Some days I struggle. The bombing infected me. I was awful afterwards. I started drifting into a dangerous, empty place. I went from bitterness to depression. It was hurtful to everyone around me. James tried hard. I didn't help myself, hence me being here. I was needing some peace.'

Diana said nothing more before Steph surprised her. 'I was brought up a Christian and was told that when you have dilemmas you should pray about it. I think it's nonsense, you don't.'

Diana unexpectedly laughed, 'Thank you.'

'You're welcome. Let's get to Sellafield.'

Diana drove on.

Six interviews in, the strain was showing. Either Kim kept to herself or they were all being protective. They claimed they knew nothing about boyfriends or drugs and according to them she was lovely and did an excellent job. The interviews were a total waste of time until the last person walked in and plonked herself in a chair, that she seemed to fully occupy. She displayed a complete arm of tattoos of random patterns and delightful skulls on each side of her neck. Steph introduced herself and asked who she was.

'Jane Simon.' was the reply, through a mouthful of chewing gum. Jane was forthcoming about being a cleaner and what a gammy job it was. About how badly she was treated by everybody that she knew, except Kim Givens, who she was at school with. She cleaned Kim's office each day, also that of her boss Mark French. He was stuck up, paid no heed to the likes of her.

'Bastard, he was rude. How can anyone be rude to me, I'm delightful.'

Diana managed to smile back. 'What about Jetty?'

'Dan Jetty. See, she did date Dan Jetty, but she dumped him. He is another total shit but useful for my medical ailments. She found a better partner. It was a couple of weeks ago. I started my shift at six after most people went home. I was cleaning the conference rooms when I heard a noise coming from French's office. Of course, being aware

of security, I thought it was my responsibility to investigate. I walked straight in the office and to my surprise I caught them in the moment their garb were coming off. He shouted at me to get out. Kim, pleaded with me to say nothing. I made myself scarce. If Jetty found out she was seeing another bloke, who knows his reaction.'

It was warm and balmy, the fading sun reflected on the rippling surface of Windermere. Steph and Fiona Collins waited on the balcony for their drinks. Diana placed three bottles of Kronenbourg on the glass topped table.

'At the moment you are the only two people I trust. We have a leak. Someone is giving information to Jetty and my bet it's

Martins. Ingles won't listen to reason. To him it's a serial killer, he's not interested in any other explanation.'

Steph spoke first. 'I agree. This doesn't smell right. First time round we found nothing in the gun clubs. Why travel all the way to the Lakes to do this? It's too much of a coincidence that Givens and Wilson are linked to Jetty. He's a more viable suspect. Gabriel Wood's killing, sadly, is to put us off the track, and keep us thinking it's a serial killer. We are searching for a hired killer.'

Collins interrupted. 'What about the guy on Blencathra that was murdered? He was doing secret squirrel stuff at Sellafield where Givens and Wilson were too. Isn't that a possible scenario? You think Jetty paid a lot to have these people killed. Where's the real motive? How would he find the hired killer? It doesn't add up at all. It's like we are playing chequers but the game is chess, it's more complicated than we imagine. It's a cluster of facts without a pattern. Don't you think?'

Steph nodded. 'We should follow both possibilities. If we put Martins on the serial killer, trawling through records, that will keep him busy and far away from Jetty. We three concentrate on Jetty and Sellafield. That way if it's not Jetty we may still get him arrested for his drug business. A way in might be Cody Beck.'

Diana knocked back her beer. 'I remember a famous anecdote about the musician, legend, Neil Young. Don't suppose you've heard him.'

Steph held up her hand.

'OMG, not the music stories again.'

'Ignoring that thank you. Well back in the 1970s he was playing the first concert of a nationwide tour. He released a surprising album, 'Tonight's the Night'. You always expect a few songs off the latest album. Neil came out and the first half was the whole of the new album, which got a muted response and eventually a lot of boos. When he came out for the second half he promised, 'I'll play a few songs you have heard before.'

The crowd cheered. What did he do? He played the whole of the album again.'

Fiona piped up. 'The point of that is?'

'We are not playing the whole of the Ingles album again, that the answer is a serial killer and nothing else. Let's sing a different song. Let's go see Cody. In the meantime keep Martins at bay by talking again to the Gun clubs. Fiona, do some background research on the chap Mark French, also whatever you can discover about the scientist Berwick Stewart. I'll ring my MI5 man to see what we can get before we go to Sellafield again. Why don't we bring Mrs Stewart into the station? Maybe a formal interview might rattle her. We may have, a hired killer by Jetty or maybe affairs going down at Sellafield.'

An hour later, Fiona left. Diana and Steph were staring out over the twilight on Lake Windermere.

'Steph, here's the thing. Why is anger red?'

Steph let out a sigh, another story about to start. 'OK I'll play along. Why is anger red?'

'It's about being on fire, brazen, it explodes, uncontrolled, laying waste, lamping any target in its way. That's how I feel about Jetty. What if anger is blue? An anger that's cold, empty, without regret, icicles finding their intended targets. What do they have in common? They are both selfish, nothing matters except the owner of the anger.'

'Fascinating. How does all this help us?'

Diana thought back to the furious eyes, the finger on the button, the blackness, the screaming, and her own desperation. It seeped in over the months, a multiplying virus, corroding her faith. Her doubts became rebukes, outbursts of temper and a desire to escape.

'Our man has blue anger. It's unfeeling, killing without remorse, killing from a distance, unconnected. I don't think that's trained into him; it's bred inside of him before he became a sniper.'

24

In the backseat

August 2nd

Three hours early morning surveillance and no-one came or went from Dan Jetty's place. The Audi smelt of chips and vinegar.

Stephanie opened the passenger door. 'Di, it stinks in here. Here's your coffee. Still nothing?'

'Not yet.'

Diana grunted with the same sullen expression from when she first picked her up. Steph slipped into the passenger seat. Ten minutes later.

'Give it a rest.'

'What?'

'You did it again. The poppysmic. That's what they call it when you purse your lips, pull them apart and this noise comes out like a sloppy kiss. It's exasperating. You do it when you're irritated.'

Diana put poppysmic into Google.

'Well I never, the noise made by smacking the lips together, thought you made it up. Where the hell did you learn that.'

'First, I am knowledgeable, second I watch movies.'

Diana was absorbed in thought staring out the car window. 'Steph, do you think you'll ever get married, have kids?'

'Married maybe, kids no. Pregnancy is another of your God's design faults like wasps and Noel Edmonds.'

'Funny, jokes aren't your thing.'

Steph was about to make a comment when a figure came around the corner and up the steps to Jetty's flat. It wasn't Jetty.

He rang the bell. After several more attempts, he turned, walking away.

'Steph, let's grab him.'

They quickened their pace towards the lone figure. At the wrong moment he turned, saw them, and started to run. They chased him in the dark, up North road, into Sweden Bridge lane, but lost him into the fields a mile further up.

Diana bent over, taking several breaths, trying to recover, before standing hands on hips,

'Damn, I didn't see him.'

'I did, that was my neighbour, Gary. A thug in the making.'

Sitting in the reception at Sellafield, Steph was trawling through the printed phone records of Berwick Stewart. Most were calls to Sellafield, some to doctors and the like until Steph reached the final two. The first was to an agency. Checking the name on Google, it was for a cottage booking in the Lakes. The second was to a London number.

'I'll be a minute Di, have to make a couple of calls.'

Before she could complain, Steph disappeared from the reception. It was a peculiar room. The pictures on the wall were all of the Sellafield site. Not the usual, landscapes, people, celebratory plaques you see in other businesses. The magazines were the same, plus the inevitable Financial Times. She smiled at the receptionist who ignored her. She'd learnt not to sit on the trendy settees.

Steph rang the agency on her smartphone. She was told that Berwick paid for a four-night stay from July 17 to July 21 for a cottage in Threlkeld. The booking wasn't just for him, it was for five people. The names given were Kate and Peter Braithwaite, Catherine and Berwick Stewart and Peter Manners.

The second number in London was unexpected. Even in these days of more transparency, she was surprised when the answer that came down the line as the offices of MI5. She explained the purpose of the call and was told that an appropriate individual would get back to her. She headed back to the reception. 'I think I found an interesting fact about our victim on Sharp Edge.'

A familiar woman walked into reception, offering a handshake. 'Inspector Petrou, how are you? We didn't get the chance to say goodbye last time.'

'Faria, pleasure to see you again and a belated thanks for your hospitality. This is my colleague DC Stephanie Giles'

Steph remained stern faced, shaking hands.

'I'm helping Mr French out; we haven't appointed a new PA yet. Is this about Kim, what's the latest?'

Steph asked. 'Enquiries are progressing. Excuse us but I need to have a quick word with the DCI.

'Faria, can you give us a minute?'

'Must warn you, Mark is busy. Go to that door on the far side when you are ready, push the buzzer, I'll come get you.'

With that she walked away.

'Well that was rude Steph.'

'You haven't forgotten she tried to get into your phone and pad. Did you hear how she switched from Mr French to Mark.'

'Is that it?'

'No, before we see French, I have found out a couple of things that might change our questions. I've been through Berwick's phone record.'

Diana listened to what Steph had discovered. 'OK. Call Collins, get her to see what she can gleam about this couple, the Braithwaites and MI5, let's see if they call back. Let's see if French has any MI5 dealings. When we get back, we'll go see Mrs Stewart. I enjoy talking to a liar. See how great a hole she will dig. Sound work Steph.'

As they reached the door, Faria reappeared, 'I'm sorry Mark has been called away, shall I make a re-arrangement.'

25

Paranoid android

August 3rd

The interview room was four bare magnolia walls, in urgent need of a repaint, without windows, lit by two overhead bulbs without lampshades. The door had two glass panes that Diana and Steph were staring through at Catherine Stewart. She was ill at ease, fidgeting in her chair, taping her foot on the floor. She took a mirror from her handbag, checking her make-up, checking each fingernail. Diana gripped the door handle.

'Steph, can you start, read Mrs Stewart her rights, then ask the first question, I'll watch her reactions.'

'OK.'

Diana sat down, placing her leather folder on the desk. Steph flicked a switch on the tape recorder and went through the formalities.

'This is an interview with Catherine Stewart, with DCI Diana Petrou and DC Stephanie Giles present, at 3:30 PM on August 3rd. Mrs Stewart, you are not under arrest, we simply need you to help us with our enquiries. The interview is being recorded; you are free to leave at any time. You may have legal representation if you think you need it.'

Catherine shook her head.

'Mrs Stewart could you say that for the tape.'

'I don't require legal representation.'

Catherine sat bolt upright and turned to Diana. 'I thought we'd dealt with it all. Why am I here?'

Diana pinned her two elbows on the desk and rested her chin on her entwined hands.

130

Steph spoke. 'Are you pregnant?'

'That's none of your business.'

Catherine crossed her arms with a defiant attitude.

'The way we see it, this is Mark French's baby. An affair is one thing, a baby is quite another, I guess a messy divorce is at the worst time and maximum embarrassment for Mr French and whatever scheme he's operating. Did you follow and kill your husband on the 20th or did Mr French arrange it?'

'This is ridiculous. OK I am pregnant. It is Mark's. A messy divorce isn't a reason to murder and I don't own your murder weapon. Alright?'

Diana and Steph let the room descend to silence. It lasted a minute before Catherine remarked. 'This is stupid. I didn't hate my husband and never desired him dead. We fell out of love. I found Mark. The idea that I could kill him in such a brutal way is preposterous.'

'OK, that means Mr French arranged it.' Diana pointed at her, 'He has an alibi but could have hired a killer. By the way, what was your alibi again?'

'I came off the fell, got into my car, drove home. I was alone, didn't make any phone calls, watched the TV, later went to bed.'

'Before you told us you went to the cottage.'

'Yes, to collect my clothes, but I didn't see anyone.'

'No alibi.'

'You have not one scrap of evidence that I did this. You have any prints or witnesses?'

Steph sensed the moment to challenge.

'You do have a motive and the weapon used is easily available. Maybe Mr French has a superior motive. An affair with the wife of a man reporting to him and getting her pregnant. If that gets out he might lose his job.'

'I can see one flaw in your argument.'

'What's that?'

'My doctor in Seascale. He didn't tell me I was pregnant till the day after Berwick died.'

131

Steph didn't react and asked, 'Were you informed what Berwick was working on?'

'No, he didn't chat about that. What was the point? It was technical detail beyond my knowledge. I can tell you it was demanding. He was engrossed in it. That was when we fell apart. Why do you ask?'

'Well if he wasn't killed for your affair, what other motivation? I ask you again, did he tell you about his research?'

'The only thing he ever said to me, it was original research he was doing which could result in a total change for the Nuclear Industry. Hardly a reason to kill him. Haven't you got a serial killer on the loose, isn't that the culprit?'

'It's one of the possibilities.'

Catherine stood up. 'As I am not under arrest, I intend to go.'

Diana stood. 'You are free to go though we may have cause to question you again. We will interview your doctor to confirm what you've told us. I suggest you think again about your alibi, and whether you have any evidence that could confirm where you were when he died. Thank you for your co-operation.'

Catherine walked out of the room. Steph turned to Diana.

'What do you think, could she have done it?'

'I don't think she did. I'm not convinced myself it's enough of a motive if she is telling the truth about the pregnancy. I think we are back with either whatever he was working on or a serial killer who totally swaps his method of killing which is unusual to say the least. We should double check again any connection with Jetty.'

'I'll get onto that. How can we find the details of his research? It must be secret. Your MI5 man might help, his death must be of interest to him.'

26

Forget her.

August 4th

Diana grabbed Cody's arm. 'Talk slower, why did Jetty want Wilson dead and where the hell have you been? You've disappeared for two weeks and we needed to speak to you again.'

'You don't get it. Wilson was Jetty's' partner, how could you not know about that? Adam Wilson and Jetty have been partners since the beginning. Without Wilson, Jetty is a nobody. Wilson put up the first funding. Still does or did, and they split the profits. You think he could afford the boat, the car, the house, the lifestyle from his crappy construction business? Jetty handles the distribution. Wilson arranges the drugs coming in, using his shipments of materials from abroad for the business.'

Cody voice was insistent and desperate.

'And I'm trying to tell you Jetty found out you interviewed me and threatened me the next day. That's your leak. So I did what I was told and went into hiding at a mate's pad and laid low. But he's gotten ruthless for some reason. Adam Wilson is out of the frame, discarded; the business has grown so much that he's done a deal elsewhere. He's got a new supplier and is handling the import himself. He doesn't wanna share the profits anymore. It all happened after a visit he made to Dublin. Can you let me go?'

Diana gripped both arms hard. 'Not yet! Why are you telling us all this?'

Cody almost spat the words out. 'He's cleaning house, he's registered I may know too much, and I bet I'm next. If I help you, can you get me off any charges and protect me and my boy, otherwise I'm going. I'm telling you he's ruthless.'

Steph came back from Cody's bedroom. 'See this, suitcases, she's already packed up to leave.'

Diana pleaded. 'OK, we can ask if we can get you protection and immunity from prosecution but I know there will be one condition. We only have your word about the business partnership, and it's only speculation on the murders. Why kill Kim Givens? It's plain Jetty hasn't the skill to commit these murders. Do you have any proof he hired someone?'

Diana let Cody go, who fumbled in her pockets for a cigarette, lit one and inhaled. 'About Kim, who knows. She was his girlfriend, dumped him a few months ago. Maybe he didn't like that and removed her and Adam at the same time. Two events at the same time, and made you think it was a serial killer. Remember, he knew their routines, knew their times out on the lake. And about a hired killer, why should I know?'

'Cody, can you dig up any paperwork that they were in business; emails, texts, bank statements to tie them together, so we can serve warrants.'

Cody sat down shaking her head. 'You're joking! Risk my life for that shit. I'm already at risk and you are asking me to go back, play along to find his secrets, you must be joking!'

Diana sat next to her. 'If you do that, we will ensure your protection, the immunity from prosecution for anything previous you've done. You can go free with a fresh identity and a brand-new house to live in, far away from here. A better deal than you are facing now.'

'If I do this, it's one time and I expect your promise in writing beforehand. By the way don't say owt to DC Martins. He's the one giving Jetty information; he's blackmailing him.'

'OK, I will go get the promise in writing and bring it back. So stay here.'

Cody nodded and they made their exit.

Outside Diana was fuming. 'Steph, I knew it was Martins, I suspected it ever since you were raided by the drugs squad, but I'm still not in on his motive. We reckon Jetty got rid of two people getting in his way. Find who he hired, which is the same investigation as if we were hunting for a serial killer and another person must have killed Stewart.'

Steph measured her words. 'Seems that way.'

'Seems that way?'

'Boss, little matter of proof that he hired a killer. You only have her word. Let's wait and see what proof she can find. Remember though, we have a Sellafield link for all three.'

'True, this scenario is the most plausible. Let's find what we need, let's get warrants, and bring him in. Let's pray we haven't put her in harm's way.'

Cody threw cash, cards, phone, and make-up into a grey handbag, waiting for Petrou to arrive. She had the evidence that proved Jetty's links with Adam Wilson.

She never heard the door. A familiar voice came from behind. 'Going away?'

Cody turned, face-to-face with Jetty. 'What are you after?'

'You should be more discrete when you blab to the Police, landed me right in it.'

Cody stepped backwards.

'What the hell are you are talking about,'

'You see Cody, DC Martins owes me a few favours, he told me what you met with Giles and Petrou. I guess they will be after me. They think I maybe a murderer. That makes me most unhappy.'

She spat words at him. 'This is stupid. Martins is winding you up. I'd never rat on you, its rubbish.'

Jetty picked up the envelope from the dressing table. 'Addressed to DCI Petrou. Let's see what's inside. Oh you have been lying, all the evidence on Adam, what am I going to do with you.'

A voice from the other room called out for his mother.

'Come on Dan, we have been mates for years, I promise I won't say owt. Don't hurt Paul.'

'See your promises are useless. I won't touch the bairn; the social services will find a superb home for him.'

Jetty came in closer. She could smell the stale beer on his breath. 'You are not going to tell anybody.'

He smiled, pulled out a serrated hunting knife from his belt; a surge of adrenaline caused his muscles to pull tight and hair follicles to stand on end. He grabbed Cody around the neck before plunging the knife into her stomach and a second into her heart. Her life faded away, spraying blood on Jetty's body, neck, and face.

The damned doorbell shrilled one more time. Steph rose from the settee. 'Alright I'm coming, hold your horses!'

At the door, she peered through her peep hole at a teenager holding a parcel and iPhone. 'Got a parcel for you. It got dumped at our address yesterday.'

'You're Gary from next door? I saw you at Jetty's place.'

Steph took the chain off before opening the door. Before she could gather her wits, she was thrown against the wall by a man dressed in black, wearing a balaclava. He grabbed her round the throat, frogmarched her into the lounge and threw her on the settee. She stared up at an automatic pistol pointed at her head.

'Hands behind your back, Gary use the plastic ties.'

Stephanie studied the man, trying to take in any minor detail. Gary held up the restraints. 'Stephanie, let me tie your hands.'

The man leant over Steph. 'DC Giles, you will terminate investigating the Givens, Wilson murders'

'What are you talking about?'

A sharp slap across the head followed before the same request. 'Leave the investigation alone. If you, don't you and your flatmate will be hurt. Here's a little taste,'

He rolled out a canvass bag on the table, revealing a selection of knives, an axe, and scalpels.

'Gary, who is this guy?'

'Do as he asks. He's threatened me and my family.'

The man stepped forward; one hand pressed against her chest the other held a scalpel against her cheek. Steph screamed when he slid the blade just over the surface of the skin. He moved the blade to her throat.

Steph closed her eyes. 'OK, OK. How can I end an investigation? I'm not in charge. That's DCI Petrou.'

The man lent on her forehead forcing her against the back of the settee. 'Don't worry about DCI Petrou. That's taken care of, find a way, otherwise you and Martine will both lose your beauty. Use your imagination, lose evidence, go on holiday, I don't care.'

He backed away, grabbed her arm, and bent back her thumb. 'They break easy, don't they? If I find you pick on poor Gary, I'll be back for you.'

With that, he picked up the roll of canvas, turned, grabbed Gary by the arm and sped out.

Steph shouted after them. In the kitchen she managed to jam the handle of the breadknife between the underside of the microwave, cutting the ties.

Diana's phone rang ten times before going to voice mail.

'Call me, I've been threatened.'

Diana appeared to be staring at the beads of sweat rolling down her arm, but her thoughts were elsewhere. Six circuits of the gym didn't quieten the turmoil. Maybe the heat of the sauna would do the trick. She wiped the seat and laid down.

A whirlpool of suspects and incidents going around that still didn't make sense. After the session with Internal Affairs, were they manoeuvring her off the case but why? But Dan Jetty was still the main suspect. Neil Denver was claiming Jetty wasn't small fry anymore, so could he afford a specialist killer? But a Sellafield link too with the autopsy showing Berwick Stewart's fall was murder. The knot in her gut told her that Catherine Stewart was hiding a secret. Her calmness showed a lack of real grief.

The intercom broke through. 'Ladies and gentlemen, the club will be closing in ten minutes, please go to the changing rooms.'

The shower could wait until she got home. Diana closed her eyes, ten more minutes of peace until there was a knock on the sauna's glass door. She rolled onto her side expecting to see Tanya the receptionist. Instead there was a tall man, dressed all in black with swept back, thick blonde hair. Diana shouted, 'What do you want?'

He said nothing. Diana got up and pulled on the door, but it was locked. He raised his hand, shaking a bunch of keys dangling from a finger. He mouthed, 'Your dead,' and walked away.

Gradually, Diana felt her panic starting, staring up at a rapidly rising thermometer. He'd disabled the thermostat. She held out her hands in front, both were shaking and her breath was quickening followed by the feeling of adrenaline surging through her body. Her heart was pounding and she shouted over and over again, 'Help!' but nobody came.

She acted on her single thought to stop the panic by bashing her head against the wooden wall. In the pain, and a trickle of blood over her cheek, some normality returned. She looked around, how to get out of here?

The glass door was far too thick to break. There was a smaller window of thick glass into the jacuzzi next door. Too thick to break with her feet or fists. She bent and examined the wooden slats under the seats. She laid out on the sauna floor, judged the distance, and kicked out with both feet. On the third attempt a slat broke in two, with a jagged edge gashing a cut down her right leg. She used her hands to pull both ends free. Taking both pieces, she swung alternately at the glass window. Nothing. The thermometer showed 115 degrees. It was now or never. She swung four times in rapid succession, bending over, gasping for breath.

A tiny crack in the centre of the pane started. She swung again directly on the spot and watched the cracks ripple out. One more swing and the glass shattered. She wrapped her towel around her arm sweeping away the splinters of glass from the frame. She doubled up the towel and laid it across the bottom of the pane. Sliding forward she could feel sharp glass ends biting at her stomach. When through, all she could do was to roll forward over some smashed glass, sticking into her back. She jumped into the jacuzzi using the back of her hands to dislodge the splinters.

At reception she found Tanya, knocked out but she felt a regular pulse, before reaching for the phone and calling Steph. 'Don't talk, listen. I'm at the gym. Someone's tried to kill me. Call for an ambulance, back up and forensics.'

'Ambulance, you badly hurt?'

'No, it's for the receptionist, let's get going.'

'I've been threatened too. A thug came to the house. I'll be on my way, arrive in ten.'

Diana found towels to put under Tanya's head with one to wrap round her own bleeding leg. She took the moment, what could she remember? His height, build, hair colour, what else? She pictured him at the door and remembered his raised hand, with the tattoo of a scorpion on the inside of his forearm.

27

God only knows.

August 5th

The door squeaked as Diana eased it open. The flat's smell was as offensive as its occupant. Diana switched on the light. The room was a mess of bottles, cutlery, and take-away cartons. Not what she expected from a man who dressed so smart.

'Where are you Dan? You pick on Giles, you pick on me, there's going to be consequences. We're here to arrest you.'

Jetty emerged from the toilet.

'I don't think I invited you in.'

Diana walked up and grabbed Jetty by his shirt collar.

'You are coming with me. You are under arrest for threatening two police officers and we want to interview you about the murder of Cody Beck. That poor woman, she didn't deserve that and her son is left without a mother. You're a real bastard. Tell me, confess you did it, stuck a knife into her chest. Did someone else tell you to threaten me and Giles, or was that all your own idea?'

The grin, the stare were well practiced 'DCI, I am my own man. I didn't threaten you. I'm not a killer. Cody was an employee of mine. Unless you have something else, let me go. I didn't kill Cody, I have no reason to, we were, what shall I say, intimate friends. You don't know this. I was the father of her son and adopted baby, so why would I hurt her?'

'Because you don't give a damn about anyone and won't let anyone put you at risk.'

'I'll say it again, I didn't kill Cody, and I haven't sent anyone to threaten you two. This is all rubbish.'

Diana's grip tightened. 'Don't lie to me. The next time you send a thug, remind him about CCTV and car plates. The man at DC Giles house was Peter Barrow, a known associate of yours, in fact convicted for dealing. We will break the lad Gary, who helped him. Again why threaten DC Giles?'

'Peter Barrow is muscle for hire, could be from any of Giles' cases. Good luck in finding any proof it was me.'

Diana could feel the anger rising.

'A coincidence that we meet with Cody, she turns up stabbed to death. Forensics will pour over her place; you will have forgotten something. You are coming with me.'

Jetty spoke. 'When was she killed?'

'Last night between eight and ten.'

'I have an alibi. I was with friends for a card game.'

'Oh yes, all fine upstanding members of the community.'

Jetty straightened his clothes, staring in defiance. 'I don't think you will arrest me, otherwise DC Martins will be arrested too. I have proof he's been buying substantial amounts of cannabis for his mother. You arrest me and tapes recording him buying the drugs will be released.

The self-satisfied smile was wiped away with one stinging smack across the right cheek.

'You don't get me at all. We have learnt all about what Martins has been up to. I'm betting he told you about Cody. He's under arrest and will rat on you like a shot to get a better deal. I hate corrupt coppers who turn on their own. We are going to the station. You will tell all and Martins can go hang. Now, explain, why you sent another idiot to try and kill me.'

'What are talking about?'

'Last night you tried to have me trapped in a Sauna, to kill me.'

'What! Look, I've never killed anyone, that includes Kim, Wilson, Gabriel, and Cody, it's not my style. Nothing to do with me.'

Jetty was quivering from the redding pain in his cheek. 'How are you going to explain this?'

'Simple, resisting arrest, from what you've done, no-one will care.'

'You have no evidence to arrest me, so I'm leaving,'

Jetty pushed Diana aside and walked towards the door. A foot slipped in his path, he crashed to the hallway floor and heard a voice he recognised.

'Got you this time.'

From the doorway, Diana smiled. 'Well done, Steph.'

Each question was followed by a check with the solicitor before the repeated 'no comment'. Questions on his drug dealing and relationships with other dealers. Until they mentioned Cody. He stuck to his alibi of being at a card game. Diana slid a single sheet of paper across the table. The solicitor picked it up, whispered in Jetty's ear and slid it back. Diana picked up the paper and waved it at Jetty.

'This is a sworn statement by DC Martins. He confesses to taking drugs from you for his mother, to providing you with information about our enquiries into you. Cody was interviewed by us. She told us about your activities. She was petrified about what you might do. Before you claim Martins is making this up, what's the reason? His career is finished. He we will be charged. You might have thought they were well hidden. We have found cannabis, quantities enough to charge you with dealing. That's two charges, corrupting a Police Officer and drug dealing.'

With that Steph read out the formal arrest and they left the room.

'Steph, we'll hold him overnight, see what any forensics gives us tomorrow.'

The microwave sang its completion of the alleged handmade lasagne, another packaged dinner. Diana tugged on the corner of cardboard, easing the lid off with a knife. She took a lager from the fridge and arranged things on a tray. Culture demanded the chosen accompaniment was Branston pickle. George Alighia was pronouncing the miseries of the day on the ten-o clock news. Later, after the meal was dispatched, it was a report on BBC North that made her sit up.

Being interviewed was Anne Manners, Minister for Energy, explaining the progress on the decommissioning at Sellafield and how they were expecting a visit from a Chinese delegation on a fact-finding tour. In the background, listening, nodding his head, smiling, was Mark French.

She switched off the TV and pondered. What if they got caught up too much in the method of the killings and not enough on the motive? Was it possible that all four murderss could be linked? What if the first two killings were decoys to send them down a rabbit hole? Berwick's murder was professional. A PA employed at Sellafield, a builder who conducted major projects and a senior scientist. Sellafield was the link. Givens and Wilson might be linked to Jetty. Would Jetty have dealings with Berwick Stewart? There was no information at all he was a drug taker.

Were there two killers operating with two distinct motives and so many people not telling the truth.

Diana knew what to do next. She dialled the London number, answered by a familiar smooth, cultured voice.

'Well this is an unexpected surprise.'

'Neil, surprises usually are.'

'Touché. What are you up to?'

'Watching the TV tonight. Mrs Manners seems impressive. Destined for higher things?'

Neil Denver went silent for a moment. 'I can't comment, that's government business, MI5 keeps its opinions to itself.'

Diana was blunt. 'If you say so.'

'I'm betting you haven't called to chat about the television.'

Diana changed tack. 'Why are the Chinese coming?'

'That was for fact-finding. They're interested in how we handle safety during decommissioning. Why is that of interest?'

'Can we talk about Berwick Stewart? I can send you the autopsy findings. He was murdered with an ice pick and thrown down the fell. Who do you think has a motive?

'No idea. We haven't been investigating it.'

Diana felt she caught Neil off guard. 'Of course you have. Tell me, what was he working on? Could it be a motive?'

'Perhaps your serial killer tried to extend his skills, a bit opportunistic.'

'Neil, I have a prominent scientist, Mark French's PA and Adam Wilson who did contracts at Sellafield, all murdered, leaving Sellafield as the one link.

'How do you know Adam Wilson was at Sellafield?'

'We have radioactive traces shared by him and Kim Givens. The link is Sellafield.'

'Or coincidence. You should appreciate that the projects going on at Sellafield are vital but all visible to public scrutiny. Don't go throwing around speculation about it linking murders without any evidence, not if other plausible explanations emerge. The news says you have arrested and questioned the drug dealer, isn't he a link?

Diana waited for a reply but there was only silence. 'The dealer has no link to Mr Stewart. You have this knack of steering people away from where they are going without them noticing.'

Neil was floundering. 'I'm suggesting that you be firmer with your facts before rummaging around at Sellafield. There are certainly other possible explanations for your murders.'

'Why get a stranger to try to kill me and a thug threaten my DC. Answer me that. It doesn't sound like a serial killer?'

With that Diana slammed down the phone. Job done; first cage rattled.

Diana listened again to the message Blackpool recorded and pondered. The forensics, this far, couldn't link Jetty to Cody's death at the crime scene and an absence of witnesses in the area. His usual coterie were, of course, providing an alibi. Martins admitted everything, including telling Jetty about Cody. He was pleading for mercy for co-operating and justifying his actions from trying to help his mother, from the pain she was in. Diana was hard-hearted. Ingles acted to minimise any embarrassment for himself. That leaves the Scorpion tattooed man at the sauna. Was this Jetty's or someone else's hired killer?

August 6th

Steph read out the date and names of those present for the tape. 'Mr Jetty you have been charged with corruption of a public official, the possession with intent to supply class A drugs. Do you have a statement to make?'

For the first time the solicitor intervened. 'My client denies these charges. DC Martins is making a false statement because of his involvement with Cody Beck and that the drugs found at my client's flat have been planted. My client has been harassed by the Police for years without any conviction of illegal activity. Mr Jetty is a legitimate businessman, importing construction materials and will make no further comment. Today I will be applying for bail. I suggest this interview is terminated.'

Diana broke into a wide smile, rocking back on her chair. 'One more thing. We took what you were wearing last night and sent them to forensics,' Diana paused, opened a folder and slid a photograph across the table. 'You recognise this?'

'Yes, it's a pendant I wear.'

'We took it from you last night.'

Diana took the photo back and waved it in her hand. 'Forensics is a wonderful thing. I guess you disposed of the clothes you were wearing when you knifed Cody, got rid of the knife, thought there was nothing to place you at the scene and a dubious group of your aimable employees to provide you an alibi. Except for this. You forgot about this chain. This chain has tiny droplets of Cody's blood that could only have happened when you stabbed here in the chest. I guess you liked the idea of staring at her when you did it. Mr Jetty you will be charged with the murder of Cody Beck.'

Jetty sat stern, impassive, silent.

Steph enquired. 'Now, I want to question you about Kim Givens, Adam Wilson and Gabriel Wood. Who did you hire to kill them?'

Jetty's expression altered. He laughed. 'You guys are incredible. I didn't kill Cody. That blood could have happened anytime. I always wear that chain. And the other murders. You're mad. Why kill Kim? What, because we broke up, I already have another girlfriend and why Adam? If I killed him my business is dead. We partner together importing construction material. He has the contacts and the transport network. Have you found anything to suggest I hired a killer? No, I didn't think so.'

Steph interrupted. 'It wasn't your only business together. He used his imports to bring in the drugs you deal.'

'No comment.'

'And the drugs were stored at Wilson's warehouse. We've searched and found traces of several class A drugs.'

Jetty's solicitor whispered in his ear, but he waved him away. Jetty thumped the table. 'Cut the crap. If drugs were in that warehouse, it was Adam's business not mine and I didn't kill him, Givens or Cody. You have no evidence, so I'm leaving.'

As Jetty stood up, Diana raised her voice for the first time. 'Sit down, I'm not finished.'

Jetty hesitated, fixing Diana with a stare of hatred, before breaking out into a smile and sitting down again.

'Mr Jetty, in the course of our investigation we found out that the Wilsons owned an old warehouse, now derelict.

'So?'

'We went there and found a burnt body. Forensics on the corpse's dental records identified the body as Mel Wilson, who's been missing for days.'

'Sounds like Adam's drug dealings caught up with the son.'

Diana pushed another photo across the table. 'You weren't as clever as you think. There were two sets of footprints left in the dust, undisturbed. We took casts and matched one set to trainers found in your apartment. Those trainers also have dust in the grooves matching the dust in the warehouse.' Diana stood up. 'Dan Jetty you are charged with the murders of Cody Beck and Mel Wilson. You do not have to say anything, but it may harm your defence if you do not mention, when questioned, something which you later rely on in court. Anything you do say may be given in evidence. Take him away.'

Back in the office, drinking coffee, Steph was talking as she was writing on the white board. 'Di, it's still a stretch for Jetty's motive to kill Givens. If he didn't do that, did he really kill Wilson and Wood, they were all killed in the same fashion. So is it still a serial killer and a co-incidence about their links to Jetty or did he hire a killer? If he did why kill Cody and Mel Wilson himself? And is there still a Sellafield connection? Back to whether we have one, two or three killers. I remember a saying my Dad used a lot, never go to sea with two compasses. Maybe we should concentrate on one theory first.'

'You're right. I need to make a phone call.'

'What's so urgent, where are we going?'
Diana put the car into gear and drove on.
'Where are we going?'
'I got a little interesting info last night. We haven't investigated Sellafield enough. I made a call,'
Steph broke in. 'Faria, I suppose.'
'Yes Faria. To cut a long story short, she is far from enamoured with her boss and suggested that he and the Minister, Anne Manners, may have a deeper relationship than we knew, and we may find out more at a hotel in Lancaster.'
'How is that linked to these killings?'
'I haven't fathomed it all yet. Mr French has become a person of interest. He was Kim Given's boss; Adam Wilson was on construction projects and Berwick Stewart reported to him. I

haven't got the answers yet but I'm gonna get to the bottom of all this. OK?'

At first, it was the coal black tresses lying on her slim shoulders and her way of flicking the strands behind each ear that signalled to anyone to pay attention. Sharp, intense brown eyes, a curved mouth, a jawline sweeping to a gentle point. Dressed to appear both smart and aloof, a black camisole below a black cashmere cardigan with gold buttons, with a recognisable knitted motif. The skirt was multicoloured in a rigid bell shape and the single piece of jewellery, small diamond earrings. Amongst the melee of dark suited, middle-aged executives in the hotel lounge, she stood out.

She walked towards Diana who guessed she was in her thirties, maybe five ten in black stilettos, with an attitude of assurance and nothing on her ring finger. She smiled extending a handshake.

'Is it DCI Petrou?'

'Yes. This is my colleague DC Giles.'

'Pleasure to meet you both. I'm Alison Black, Hotel Manager. How can I help? Can I get you both a drink?

Pleasantries were exchanged as three tonic waters were delivered; Diana spoke. 'We thought we should speak to you in person. This is a delicate matter. It's linked to investigations we have ongoing and concerns guests staying here some time ago.'

Diana expected protestations about privacy. Alison took one sip of her drink, crossed her legs, staring at both of them in turn, before speaking in her soft Irish tone.

'Why don't you explain what you are investigating, and I can see if I can help.'

Steph held a photo. 'Do you recognise this gentleman?'

'I do, that's Mr French from Sellafield, he uses our conference facilities for business meetings and larger conferences.'

'A key question. Was he here on May 15th?'

A phone call established Mark French made a booking that day and stayed the night too.

Alison stood up. 'Is that all.'

Steph stood too. 'That's not all. Please sit down. Your manager assured us of your full co-operation?'

Alison's smiling demeanour slipped away behind a barrier of crossed arms. Diana spoke holding up a photo. 'Was this woman staying here that night?'

Alison's hand covered her mouth. She tried to speak in a whisper. 'Put that down. That's Anne Manners, Minister of Energy, you can't expect me to divulge anything about her,'

She stood, shook her head, and strode out of the lounge. Steph went to follow. Diana mouthed. 'Wait.' Alison returned a few minutes later, sat down, gazing backwards and forwards at the two detectives, rubbing her fingertips with her thumbs, sighing.

'OK. My boss tells me I have to co-operate. I have checked the bookings. She did stay, that night.'

Diana leaned forward, noticing Alison's hands were shaking. 'You can guess my next question, and I want a truthful answer. Did they stay in the same room?'

'Maybe. They have been back since.'

Diana asked. 'Has Mr French promised you a reward for your discretion?'

'No. All Sellafield business meetings and conferences have always been held here for years in case that's what you are thinking.'

Diana pressed on. 'Still, it's a perfect little arrangement he has, a discrete site to carry on his affairs and you ensuring his privacy. Last question, and if I get straight answer I won't tell your boss what you've been up to. Who else?'

Fidgeting in her chair, Alison quietly said, 'A Mrs Stewart and once his PA.'

Diana's parting words to Steph were on voice mail. 'Don't forget I'm going back to the city tomorrow for the Inquest. In the

149

meantime, research French and these liaisons with Mrs Stewart and Givens.'

At home she dialled a number on speaker phone and didn't wait for a response. 'Were you told about Anne Manners and Mark French?'

'Greetings Diana.' Neil Denver replied. 'How are you?'

Diana posed the question again with expletive emphasis. Neil was curt. 'What about them?'

'Our information is they are having an affair.'

A silence before a surprising reply.

'Not certain if you would call it an affair. Diana, do you have any concept of what we try to achieve with people. I'll tell you it's leverage. That's our game. I suggested to Mark French that our Minister of State, might be flattered and seduced by a handsome, tall, fit, unattached man. We have the leverage with the pictures we obtained.'

Diana said, 'What's the leverage for?'

'She's the latest Minister of Energy. Like all Ministers they like to be seen to doing things and we don't want her getting any ideas about changing plans at Sellafield, the decommissioning task is too important and has to proceed on plan. This has nothing to do with your murders. Leave this investigate alone, and don't go near either of them. The threats and attempts on your life, that's your drug dealer. I can assure you MI5 has nothing at all to do with those, it's not how we operate.'

'Why should I believe you?'

Silence followed, before the retaliation came.

'Diana, you have forced me into this. I can use the evidence we have to stop your investigation. I guess no-one told you. We were given the surviving CCTV from outside the stadium the day Affredi set off the bomb, retrieved by forensics on the day. Our objective was more info on Affredi, his bomb, trigger device but didn't expect to find what you did. It shows your movements that day in glorious colour.'

'Where are you going with this.'

'Oh Diana, you have been trading on your hero status ever since. Not the hero eh. You lied to the investigators, to colleagues, media, and to yourself. The video shows the secret you have been harbouring and how your breakdown came about, playing the Christian with the wracked conscience.'

An answer didn't come. Just silence down the phone.

'I suggest you drop any investigation into Sellafield, into the Minister. Go back to your serial killer or the drug dealer. Take my word, Sellafield is not involved in these murders, not involved in any actions against you. If you don't stop the CCTV tapes will see the light of day.'

'You must be desperate to resort to blackmail.'

The retort was sharp and loud.

'Damn right, stay away from Sellafield! Watch what you say tomorrow at the inquest.'

The signal went before Diana could speak.

February 2019

Diana met Neil Denver whilst minding her own business drinking in the Panorama Bar, high above the city. It was a grey winter's day, which did nothing to enhance the mood. Diana was mulling over her future. She was out of step with all her colleagues. Her own morals didn't square with what they thought was acceptable to get the job done. Her saving grace was being smarter. Her thoughts were interrupted when Neil Denver sat down, uninvited, and declared they should talk. That was the first she heard about a potential bombing in the City from chatter picked up, linked to the visit by the PM. He suggested a co-ordination on security. What Diana couldn't believe was that they identified three terrorists but expected them watched but not picked up in case they might lead to the real instigators. How wrong that went.

How could they risk the PM's life? Her Boss was adamant it was down to MI5 and the PM herself agreed. It needed three teams of six round the clock on each suspect. They dismissed the theory it could be an attack anywhere else. She told them that it was the latest shopping centre launch and a derby game. They agreed to beef up the security at each, nothing else and keep the suspects under intense surveillance.

Diana remembered the call came after 2:00pm. A video was released by the third target, Michael Affredi, talking about killing adults and children. Worse the surveillance team lost him, on Queen Street. That was away from the shopping centre, but minutes from the football stadium.

Diana remembered the fear that racked her body weaving her Mini in and out of traffic on Yorke Way. She drove into Queen Street and a lorry backed out unexpectedly. She hit the brakes hard, and the car slid sideways into the lorry. Her body whipped from side to side She fumbled with the seat belt, finally getting it undone. She fell onto the road, got to her feet, started to run, leaving a string of obscenities in her wake.

Five minutes later, the impressive new Football Stadium came into view.

28

Electioneering

August 7th

'Morning Steph, where are you?'

'In the office, where are you?'

Diana went silent for a moment, negotiating the VW up a slip road. 'On my way to the Inquest about the February bombing, appearing at 1:00 PM. I have things for you to do today. You might get Collins help and keep Martins at arm's length till we can interview him.'

'What do you want done?'

'I've been thinking again about Castle. Let's make sure we have that all properly tied off. Too much focus on this investigation for any repercussions afterwards, any sense that we didn't investigate to the full extent. Check his movements again, see if he has any alibi at all or if anyone saw him at the time of the murders. Check his neighbours, anyone who knew him at the Gun Club and see if he has any relatives hereabouts. I learnt he didn't have a mobile, double check his landline.'

An annoyed, exasperated voice interrupted the flow. 'Di, this is ridiculous. That's a ton of wasted effort when we should be following up on Jetty and finding out what's happening at Sellafield. The letter sealed it. He didn't do it. You knew that yourself. Who's putting pressure on you? Is Ingles making us do this.'

'No! We are going to be thorough. Do more checks on Jetty. He may have needed to kill Givens and Wilson. We haven't found out why yet. Hiring a killer is an expensive business. How might he go about it? Let's lean heavy on his dealers, check all his finances.'

'Who is going to do all this?'

'We are, you, me, Collins, and anyone else we can drag in. I'll get help from my previous nick, if needed. If it is a serial killer, it could be Castle but there may be other possibilities we haven't unearthed. Go back over all the possible suspects and maybe we will get a breakthrough from Pathology. Chase up Blackpool. These are our priorities. We leave Sellafield out of it for the moment. Have you got all that?'

Steph held the phone away in a failed attempt to hold her annoyance.

'Steph, do you hear me?'

'This is bloody ridiculous after last night. All we have found out about Sellafield and French says we should investigate further and not waste our time on Castle. Who's got to you?'

The line went dead, followed by the sound a phone crashing against an office wall.

The Coroner was unusual, being a woman in her thirties. Tall, elegant, in a long, plain, navy dress. She read from notes on a tablet to the assembled witnesses and media, dwarfed by the towering stone wall of the Stadium's East Stand. Emblazoned on the wall, a twenty-foot-high team crest was scarred and blackened, forever commemorating the dead fans. She pointed to the crest, reminded the assembled people that this was the spot where the bomb exploded and requested a minute's silence.

'Ladies and Gentlemen, excuse the alternate venue for this inquest. It was felt, given the structure of today's hearing that this was the most appropriate location. A specific list of witnesses, from those in command in the Police, MI5, and emergency services will be called to testify, but the first witness will be DCI Diana Petrou.

Diana stepped forward. Each stride weighed heavy under the burden she carried. She stood a few feet away from the Coroner, hiding her shaking hands behind her back.

'DCI Petrou, can you tell us about your designated role on February 23rd?'

Diana drew her feet together, notebook in her right hand, elevating her head before speaking. 'I was leading the deployment of our Police resources on the streets in liaison with my central command and MI5.'

'Why were MI5 involved.'

'MI5 gained intelligence about a possible bombing that day and the PM was due to deliver a speech. All her security detail were present. They identified three possible suspects.'

The Coroner made an aside to the assembly. 'Other witnesses will provide testimony on other matters leading up to the 23rd. I will spend our time with DCI Petrou, in this appropriate location, to better understand the events of that day. DCI Petrou, in your written statement after the bombing, you described driving through the city and but approached the stadium on foot.'

'That's correct.'

'You were given intelligence that Mr Affredi was the bomber and was heading here. What was the intelligence?'

Diana's lips tightened and notebook in hand, she began. 'A video recorded by Mr Michael Affredi was released at 1:00 PM, describing his intention to kill hundreds, without mentioning the target. Using face recognition technology he was discovered on CCTV in Vermont Road, ten minutes' walk from the stadium.'

'What happened next?'

'All officers on duty were dispatched to the stadium and man all the entrances.'

The Coroner interrupted. 'But where you.'

'When I received the call, I was driving into Queen Street.' Diana cleared her throat before continuing. 'I drove into Queen Street at high speed with blues and two. A lorry was reversing across the road. I braked, slid sideways. The passenger side collided into the lorry. I was shaken about but managed to get out of the car and ran.'

The Coroner turned, peaking over her glasses. 'Were you hurt? Were you concussed?'

'No. I was shaken up, some bruising from my seat belt but was able to run.' Diana returned to her notes. 'I ran from Queen Street into Redlands Road, before turning into the concourse in front of the East Stand. It had two turnstile entrances, each down to queues of twenty to thirty with the game already started.'

The Coroner held up her hand to pause Diana, so she could make notes on her tablet. 'How did you spot Mr Affredi?'

'We were sent a frame from the CCTV images,' checking her notes, 'He was dressed in blue jeans, white trainers, a plain, bright red hoody over a white T Shirt.'

'How far away were you at this time?'

Diana examined her notes. 'About thirty feet away. One man's clothes matched the description given and he was halfway down the first queue, which was moving forward through the turnstiles.'

The witnesses were attentive and the reporters scribing. The Coroner caught the moment. 'Where were you exactly?'

'I hid myself behind the last person in the queue.'

'DCI Petrou,' Diana knew the question to come, 'What was your next step and were you armed?'

The notebook was flipped shut. 'I was armed, for that day, with a Police issue Glock 17 Semi-Automatic pistol.'

The Coroner was concentrating on the assembly in front. 'Now this is most pertinent DCI Petrou. What did you do next?'

'I drew my weapon and stepped one pace to the right of the queue till Affredi was in line of sight, so I could shoot with the lowest risk to others.'

'What were your instructions from your Command if you found him, was it to arrest him?'

The whole focus turned to Diana. A moment's silence. 'My instruction was to shoot on sight. He kept his hood up. I couldn't see his face but his clothing matched our information and he was the right height and build. I called out his name. He turned to face me, confirming it was him, I shot; he fell. A trigger device was attached to his thumb which he pushed before he died. The bomb went off.' Diana felt a rush of shame, she'd never lied on oath before.'

The Coroner gestured to quell the murmur from the crowd. 'Your next recollection?'

'Mayhem. Being a little distance away, I was thrown backwards by the blast and showered with smithereens that tore through my clothes and skin. Eight people immediately around him in the queue were killed. Others died later from their wounds and a number survived but with life changing injuries.

The Coroner interrupted. 'This is vital. Are you convinced you did shoot him? Did you miss, giving him time to press that button?'

Diana feigned indignance and stood up straight. 'I am a trained officer to carry a firearm. I shot him in the chest.'

'This was a stressful situation. Understandable you may have panicked. You had been in a car crash, maybe exhausted from the chase?'

Diana exclaimed. 'No! I wasn't out of breath, I shot, I hit him, I killed him.'

The Coroner made a side comment. 'Given the strength of the blast and destruction of Mr Affredi's body the Pathology was unable to determine that; we only have your word. The bullet was destroyed in the aftermath. DCI Petrou, how do you account for not dying yourself?'

'I had on a bullet proof vest that protected my torso and so only my legs and arms were cut. I saw his thumb press the button so was able to dive to the ground and cover my head. The action of the paramedics and surgeons meant I didn't lose a limb.'

The Coroner spoke out. 'DCI Petrou thank you for your testimony today. It is tragic that many people lost their lives. Your conduct may have saved hundreds from preventing the bomb going off on the crowded terraces. The people of the City owe you a debt of gratitude.'

At home, she didn't speak all through a late lunch and an uneasy atmosphere commanded the room. Afterwards she went for a walk with Jack in the park. In the hazy afternoon heat they sat on a park bench, with two 99s, watching life go by.

'Mum.'

'Yes.'

'I have a question?'

'Should I be worried?'

Jack leant forward staring at the ground.

'You've always brought us up to be honest, that's what we get in Sunday School.'

'Where's this going?'

'You remember my best mate Graham. He got detention from the Head for swearing in class at Miss Evers. I was with him later, when he used a coin and made a scratch all the way down the side of the Head's car. I just watched him. He told me he'd beat me up if I told on him.'

Diana nodded.

'The next morning, in assembly, the Head asked for anyone who knew about it to come and talk to her. Later, when leaving, Graham grabbed me and threatened again to beat me up if I told tales and everyone would be told I was a grass. Mum, I've said nothing.'

Diana put her arm around her son. 'What do you think you should do.'

'I should admit it wasn't right what he did. But I can't fight Graham, he's way bigger than me.'

Diana stood up. 'My suggestion, go to Graham, offer him the chance to own up himself, own up to what he did, admit rather than get found out. My experience if you own up the punishment is way less than if you are found out. If he's found out he might be expelled.'

'He's stronger than me. I'm scared about what he can do.'

'Go tell the Head, tell her your worries about what might happen to you. Dad or I can come with you, and make sure the Head tells this boy the consequences of hurting you.'

Back in the house, James pulled up a chair in front of Diana. He handed over a white wine.

'OK, tell me what it is.'

Out of character, tears flowed, fingers locked tight together. The hypocrisy of her advice to her son, the shame she felt about lying under oath for the first time in her career.

After a deep breath, Diana eventually spoke. 'James, I need to tell you what happened at the bombing. I gave Jack some advice I haven't taken myself. I don't know if I can still call myself a Christian.

With that, the whole true story tumbled out. It was the first time since the bombing she had told anyone. James hugged his wife tight as Diana sobbed.

From a distance, Diana watched her running a finger around the rim of the gin glass. Putting things right starts with this woman. She thought about her in last night's TV interview. Her desire to achieve and to be lauded, came across more than any sense of service. She was a believer that nothing matters more than success. After six years in Parliament, Anne Manners was already a Minister of State, attracted by power and now Diana knew she was having an affair with French.

Success bought expensive outfits, which tried to hide an expanding girth. Dark hair, styled into a bob around her cheeks, with narrow brown eyes and thin lips. What did French see in her? Her expressions ran the gamut from disappointment to disdain as she fended off her entourage bringing questions and papers.

Diana tracked her down to this constituency meeting in Morecambe. She flashed her warrant card to her minder and strolled over, sitting in an adjacent seat.

'Minister, I spent last night chatting to Neil Denver at MI5. He suggested we talk. I'm DCI Petrou.'

She turned. 'I doubt he said that at all. I recognise you. You're the hero of the bombing in February, the bomb that we thought was for the Prime Minister. What now, I'm busy?'

'I interviewed your husband Peter yesterday; he was staying at a cottage in Threlkeld with a man called Berwick Stewart who was murdered on Blencathra.'

She took a mouthful from a gin glass.

'The murdered man was a scientist at Sellafield working for Mark French. Have you come across Mr French?'

'I've met him. He's the CEO or is it COO? I get lost in the acronyms. He has introduced himself a couple of times on Sellafield visits. Can't help you with this Berwick fellow.'

'He died falling from Sharp Edge on Blencathra. He was murdered and he was the chief scientist on the key projects at Sellafield, including the decommissioning. You must've met him.'

Another of her entourage interrupted, she scrawled a signature. 'Where were we? No, he hasn't been brought to my attention. I will get my advisor to investigate. Sounds like an episode I should hear about.'

Diana sensed a moment. 'Mr Stewart was staying at a cottage with his wife Catherine, your husband and the Braithwaites. Do you know them?'

'Again, no. My husband has been a walker all his life. He has an established group of fellow walkers but not my thing. I'm far too busy. I wish I could help you more.'

With that, she downed the remains of the G&T and ambled off. Diana thought, 'Lies come easy to her, like mercury sliding over glass.'

Stuck for three miles behind the Ambleside bus, Faria's agitation was morphing into recklessness. At least she was through the centre of Ambleside. Thirty more minutes down to

Windermere and escape on the train. One visit on her way to hand over the material. Her hands sweated on the wheel and her skin prickled with fear. She chose the wrong moment to overtake. Headlights were bearing down on her and both vehicles swerved, brakes squealing. Faria crashed into a parked car on the side of the road. The airbag saved her life. She felt the agony in her neck and her legs. The sudden taste of acidic smoke hurried her exit from the car. Out of the car she felt the blood seeping down her bare leg, from a gash where she had caught the bent metal of the door frame. She heard shouts behind her but panicked and tried to run. The pain shot up her leg at each step, and blood was seeping into her shoe. Ten minutes down the road she saw the sign to the Low Wood Resort. Thank goodness. She peered at the name plates before pressing the bell for apartment ten.

Diana peered at the screen.

'Please let me in, I'm injured.'

Faria stepped back and showed the blood running down her calf. Diana pushed the buzzer. She met her halfway up helping her up the stairs into the apartment. She felt Faria's body shaking as she helped her walk to the sofa.

'I'll clean this up.'

She disappeared into the kitchen hunting for the first aid box. From the sofa Faria was still saying thank you. Diana could see the frailty, the fear in her eyes. She began cleaning the leg with antiseptic wipes. 'What the hell has happened?'

'I crashed my car and ran here. I was on my way to see you. You are a life saver.'

'I'll call this in. Where's your car?'

'No Police, he mustn't find out or know where I am. Can I stay here tonight, return the favour?'

'Who's after you?'

'Mark, Mark French, he's behind it all.'

Diana touched the wound. Faria let out a cry of pain. 'That's a real cut I expect it needs stiches.'

'I'm leaving, going back to Germany, to a country where he doesn't think I'm a threat. Please bandage this up and I'll get it fixed when I am far away from here.'

Diana bandaged the leg and gave her pain killers. 'Can you tell me what is going on?'

Faria handed over a flash stick. 'It's vital you keep this safe. Make copies. I've risked a lot to get this.'

'What's on this?'

'I wish I understood it. It's full of mathematical formulae and technical language. All I know is that this was the secret research Berwick was working on that got him killed. But I still don't know why.'

Diana rolled the flash stick around in her hand. 'What should I do with this.'

'I'm not too certain but you may need it as evidence or as leverage.'

'Faria, I'm confident French is involved in fraudulent dealings.'

'Diana understand who you are dealing with. He has a charming personality but there's no remorse for any of his actions. He sees the world as corrupt and hypocritical. I know, I fell for the charm and now he's having an affair with Catherine Stewart.'

'I've got MI5 trying to warn me off.'

'Yup, he's tight with that man Neil Denver. I've tried to tell Catherine Stewart that he only cares about one person, himself, but she didn't listen. Enough about him. The flash stick has some other files you might find interesting; invoices, emails. I think you will find that he is in cahoots with Ingles too, so if you report to him, you will be vulnerable.'

Diana nodded, disappeared to the kitchen, coming back with two glasses and a bottle of Rioja.

Faria knocked back the first in one go and held out for more. 'Diana, this whole thing is a mess. I don't think you will ever get him convicted, he's too protected. That's why I'm off to Germany.'

'I suggest you stay tonight and I'll help you in the morning with a lift to Windermere. Tell me what else you have found out.'

Faria sat up, pulling a cushion behind her back. 'I can tell there's you more than the decommissioning going on. That's what is public knowledge. It's all wrapped up with Berwick's research that's on that flash stick. He has been involved on a secret project for months with Mark, your MI5 man, and Anne Manners. They've carried on a series of conversations behind closed doors. I was barred too from the Chinese visit. The day before Berwick was killed, he and Mark were having a loud argument. All I heard when I entered the room was Berwick saying, 'This should be shared.'

Mark told him, 'Never gonna happen.' Berwick stormed out, went to his office, grabbed his papers and his laptop, and left the building. That was the last I saw of him. Today, when I knocked on Mark's office door and went in he was on the phone and screamed at me to get out. I went to Kim's desk to listen in on the call. I didn't recognise the other voice. Whoever it was, he was apologising to Mark, saying it was a mistake trying to make it seem like an accident. Mark turned round and saw me on the phone. His cold stare told me I'd been found out. When the call ended, he trudged over to me and said, 'You're finished.' I got out.'

29

Tomorrow never knows.

August 8th

The doorbell rang. Diana pulled the door ajar. Steph barged straight in.

'I saw you drive off with Faria and come back alone.'

'Are you spying on me.'

'No, I was just coming to see you about something I found. By the way, your bacon's burning. I'm mad at you. All this nonsense about Castle and ignoring Sellafield.'

Steph sat down on the sofa. 'You're about to blow this case. I thought better of you. I really thought I'd found a governor who wasn't corrupt, but I find Faria from Sellafield here. You let a suspect stay the night in your flat. How does that look? Is that why Sellafield's off limits, to protect her? Is she threatening you?'

'She knocked on my door last night. She'd been in a car crash was bruised and bloody. I fixed her up.'

'You didn't ring anybody! Why?'

'She was on the run. She told me that French threatened her. He's been having secret meetings with Anne Manners and Neil Denver. She did admit trying to get into my phone and pad on his instructions but doesn't know what he was looking for. She's really scared of him, so today she's headed back to Germany. I am not protecting anyone. She's done nothing to be arrested for, apart from leaving the site of an accident. In return for letting her go to Germany she's left us a flash stick and some papers and a story to help us. OK?'

'Alright. They found the crashed car last night. I knew it was hers, from letters in the glove box. What's on this flash stick?'

'She claims it's secret research that was done by Berwick Stewart, tied to work at Sellafield that only French, Denver and Manners know about. I thought I should know more so I looked up an idiots guide on Nuclear Power on Google.'

'Not Wikipedia I hope.'

'No it was a government site. I hadn't understood why we stopped developing more nuclear power.'

'Enlighten me.'

'In the fifties the first stations used fusion where the fusion of particles together released energy. The problem was the conditions and energy needed didn't produce much excess energy and the whole thing wasn't cost efficient. The next generation used fission where particles were split apart which produced far greater quantities of energy but also isotopes that can be used in nuclear weapons. But the real problem was how the radioactive waste was to be disposed. It takes hundreds of years to become harmless and that comes at a cost financially and potentially environmentally. Cut corners and you get at Chernobyl.'

'So what's changed?'

'Berwick did something to change this, but Faria didn't know what. Only that it prompted new construction and revenue for the government. But the answer is on the flash stick.'

Faria Engel, thirty-three years old and five feet five of impatience, was limping over the train platform, heels clicking on the stone floor. Hoping she was escaping this shallow, beleaguered outpost, of middle-aged men in drab M&S garments, with stomachs like sleeping puppies over belted trousers. Most of all, away from Mark French before she was swept up in the inevitable consequence of his scheming. Boarding the train, her brown eyes took one last dismissive regard with a mental scream of 'good riddance.'

Anne Manners adjusted her designer jacket and paraded into Sellafield, in a tight Valentino skirt which hardly flattered her figure. Anne was used to always getting what she wanted that included having Mark French all to herself and divorcing Peter. She assumed he was attracted by her power and her ability to take it away from others. Peter didn't match her ambitions. If it worked out with the Chinese, with Mark's help, being Minister for Energy was her next step.

For Seascale it was an attractive isolated house, with a clifftop view over the sea. There were no neighbours to see what Steph was doing. The sixth key opened the lock. The door squeaked. She called out, 'Police,' to see if anyone else was there. The house had been searched after Berwick's murder from top to bottom but nothing was found. Steph still hunted around all the downstairs rooms. Upstairs she entered Berwick's study. The search showed that his phone, his laptop, and his notes, were all removed. But by who? Diana for some reason knew it was MI5. Did that make sense?

Steph stood still, peering around the room. Maybe this was pointless. What was out of place? Framed awards, photos of his wife, pictures of fells, a bookcase of technical tomes, a Newton's cradle, and a printer. She pulled books away from the shelves and pulled out all the drawers of the desk and filing cabinet. Nothing was attached to them. She sat for ten minutes in the revolving desk chair scanning the room, until one thing caught her eye. Steph checked her watch. The wooden, square Habitat clock showed a time that was hours behind. Behind the clock, in the space for the battery, was a flash stick.

The pastor's office had only room enough for two people and was a ramshackle of papers, piles of books, and children's artwork stuck to the walls. Diana squirmed in a battered armchair. Ray handed over a coffee in a mug proclaiming Agnus Dei and waited for Diana to talk.

She cleared her throat. 'When we met last you tried to get me to talk about what had happened but I ran out, because it wasn't easy.' Ray shuffled forward on his office chair. 'It rarely is, but this is a safe place.'

'It's about the bombing on February 23rd. How much have you heard about it?'

'What I've seen in the papers and on social media. I believe you killed a terrorist and saved lives before he was going to set off a bomb on the terraces. It must have some after-effects.'

'Yeah. I'm suffering from PTSD from the injuries and things I saw.' Diana took another gulp of coffee. 'You'll have to bear with me. PTSD is not the real damage I am carrying; I'll tell you what did happen.'

Diana related everything up to the point where she caught up with Affredi.

Ray leaned forward. 'What happened next?'

'My orders were to shoot on sight.' There was a pause, Diana's head dropped and quietly she said. 'I didn't.'

'Didn't what?'

'I couldn't shoot. I've never killed anyone before.'

Ray waited for Diana to look up. 'You hesitated, that would be understandable.'

'No. I convinced myself it was wrong, maybe it was the sixth commandment. I shouted out his name and told him to get on his knees. He turned and set off the bomb and I shot too late.'

'I'm so sorry.'

'Sorry's not good enough. Because of my cowardice eight people immediately died, others died in hospital, and many, including me, were maimed for life.' Diana took a deep breath. 'I can't stand the shame any longer, I can't bear the memories. Worse, is what I said afterwards.'

'What did you say?

'The questioning started by MI5 the next morning and I lied. I told them I shot Affredi but he still manged to press the button. The press reported me as a hero because he never reached the terraces. I've chained myself with lies. I've lied to my family, lied to an inquest and worst of all, lied to those grieving families.'

'But you can rectify that.'

'It's not that simple. MI5 have CCTV that survived the blast which apparently shows exactly what I did that day. Someone is now blackmailing me to keep me quiet about a case I am investigating here. I've always been an honest copper. I've never bent the rules and always tried to act in accordance with my faith. Why would God forgive all this?'

The silence was dense and unnerving.

Ray said gently, 'You've been a Christian most of your life. You must know you don't come to the Lord for quick fixes but you can come to him for forgiveness and guidance.

'I don't think so.'

'Diana, God is not going to judge you for not killing someone. Your terrorist killed those people, which was his decision.'

'Why do I feel as bad as I do?'

'Diana, this is a spiritual battle too. The devil is real, and he desires nothing more than what you are putting yourself through.

'I was the one who didn't shoot, that was my decision. I disobeyed an order.'

Ray spoke again. 'I say again, the terrorist set off that bomb and killed those people. But your anguish now is to do with the lies you've told and that now needs to be out in the open.

'What should I do?'

'You have little option but to tell the truth. Some people may not comprehend, some may hate you, but the lies have to end otherwise you won't be able to move on. You may still feel responsible but it's what you do going forward that matters.'

Diana stood up and walked out of the office. Ray sat on his own and prayed for her, surprised when Diana walked back in the room and sat down again.

'I know you are right. I read somewhere that true repentance shuns evil itself more than the external suffering or shame. My hope for anything at the moment doesn't spring eternal. It's like one of those geysers which explode at random and collapse as soon as they appear. I think I know what to do for the best.'

'Tell me.'

' First, I'm going to ignore the blackmail and chase down the evidence.'

'And then?'

'I'll write to the chair of the inquest and admit my lies and provide the correct evidence. That will be the finish of my career. I have a colleague who means a lot to me, who I trust implicitly. I will have to tell her everything. I suspect by ignoring the blackmail, they will leak my fabrication to the press and give them the CCTV they have.

30

Lucky

August 9th

Diana drove her VW carefully round the hairpin bends heading towards Sellafield and a meeting with Mark French. She thought about the conversation yesterday and the actions she promised. She had already written to the Coroner at the Inquest. She had also emailed Neil Denver and made it clear she wouldn't be blackmailed. She was now determined to find out the truth.

'I'll get coffee organised. How do you take it?'

'Thanks, with just a splash of milk.'

Diana circled the office, after French walked out, waiting for the footsteps to fade away. It was a square room with featureless walls on two sides and a glass wall facing out over Sellafield and a half glass view back into the office of workstations, where people were glued to their monitors. The view over the site was a mixture of cranes, rubble, concrete buildings surrounded by heavy machinery and men slaving in the heat of the afternoon.

She walked behind the wooden desk and tested the drawers. The first was just pens and stationery, the second was locked. The third, bottom drawer, was a pile of papers but underneath was a framed black and white photo of a group of men and women, maybe twenty or more, in different uniforms. The uniforms showed various country insignia and underneath a name plate saying, Bosnia, the UN team. She stared at the photo to find French. He was in the back row with his arm round a man's shoulders. She studied the image before dialling Steph's number.

'Don't talk, just ring me back in five minutes.'

Footsteps approached the door. She threw in the photo, knocked the drawer closed with her knee and turned to a wall of certificates on safety and awards. She focused in on a picture of French in a tuxedo accepting a glass reward, underneath the label which read AEA May 2018.

French strolled in smiling with two cups in hand. 'I see you have found the photo of our reward for excellent performance on safety.'

Diana walked back round the desk to take the offered coffee. 'I gather you were in the Army.'

French put his coffee down. 'Yes. Served for twenty years. A stint in Ireland, time in Germany and finally in Bosnia. We did a fine job there. We saved lives and put away terrorists who committed horrific crimes. Afterwards I was redeployed to Germany. I resigned in 2004 and ended up here.'

Diana sipped her coffee. 'Can I ask you about Kim Givens? She was the girlfriend of a known criminal, Dan Jetty. Did she ever mention him or talk about him to you?

'You may find this incongruous detective, but as I told you last time, I try to not to engage with the personal life of the people who are assigned to me. I like to keep my own relationships strictly private and I expect the same from them. Unlike others, I don't indulge in social media. I told you before, your best bet about Kim is all the other people who knew her.'

Diana took another mouthful.

'She never gave you an indication that she was in trouble. She never seemed concerned or worried?'

'Well, I did have occasion to tell her off about the standard of her efforts. She was making more mistakes in my calendar. She did say she was worried about her mother. I offered her a few days off but she said she was okay.'

Diana's mobile rang. 'Steph what is it?'

Diana mouthed her apologies at Mark and nodded her head several times, 'Okay, I'll be on my way, should be with you in under an hour.'

171

Diana feigned annoyance. 'That was my DC, they need me back in Windermere. Can we make a rearrangement?'

French offered a business card. 'Of course, email me when it suits you and I can see what fits my calendar.'

'Thank you for all your help. I'll find my own way out.'

She hurried out of the building to the car park, before ringing Steph back. 'I'm convinced it's not Jetty and it's not drugs. It's French. He has an army picture in his office, with his arm around a man. I am sure it's the same man who tried to kill me in the sauna. He has the same tattoo of a scorpion I saw that night.

'You might be right. Don't go mad. I searched Berwick's house; on a hunch we might find material that the first search missed. I found a flash stick, well hidden. I'm intrigued to see what's on it. I'll see you back at your flat.'

From his office window French watched Diana drive away. Looking down, the bottom drawer was left ajar. He looked inside, the black and white photo was sitting on top of the contents. He dialled a speed number on his mobile.

'I've made a mistake. She's seen you in a photo in my office, she's going to make the connection. It's time to leave. Do whatever is necessary to clean up any evidence.'

The phone flashed the expected name.

'Blackpool. At last. Do you have an answer? Steph is here with me.'

'It's taken some time. I got obsessed because I hate dead ends. Our killer made a mistake. I decided to look at the bullets again. For the first killings, the bullets were wiped clean. I examined again the one in Gabriel Wood. It has a partial print. It's not enough for 100% match but enough for a probability. I did a search on the Ident1 database and drew a blank. Your said to me that you have to be an expert to make those shots. The two options were, either a skilled amateur, maybe from a gun club, or a military man. All military personnel are fingerprinted for identification in case their bodies are disfigured or injured. I have

172

sent the partial print to the M.O.D. They've promised to get back to me tomorrow.'

'Let's put a name to a fingerprint.'

Diana clicked off her mobile. 'OK. It's becoming more straightforward. We have Sellafield's chief scientist murdered on Sharp Edge leaving a hidden flash stick. Three people shot from a distance on Windermere, two of whom were employed at Sellafield. Faria's on the run because French is threatening her life. Jetty is adamant about not hiring a killer and Berwick Stewart was certainly unknown to him.'

'YES! Diana, we have a match, with a high probability. It's on the Army database. The fingerprint belongs to a man who served with a Bosnia group, as part of the UN force in 1995. His name is Vokovic. His record shows he was a sniper, trained by us!'

'Blackpool. Brilliant. Got him! Did they let on where he is?'

'He's living down in Siena. You will have to contact Italian Police to help. I've sent you all the details including this man's picture. You can put out an APB. I tried to unearth more details, but the Army didn't or wouldn't reveal any information. My guess, we have an episode which has to be kept secret, I can't tell you about anyone else in the unit.'

'A picture in French's office, shows it was his unit. This man was in his command. He killed Givens and Wilson. But I still can't see the motive. The betting is he killed Stewart too. Blackpool, you've cracked it. Thank you. I owe you a drink.'

Diana found Steph by the coffee machine. 'You want one?'

'No, nor do you. Blackpool's been on the phone. He has a breakthrough. I'll fill you in with the details on the way. We need to plan how we put French in the frame.'

He never heard the man walk in or pick up a scalpel. Vokovic grabbed Blackpool round the neck pulled his arm up behind his back, twisted him around and pointed the scalpel straight at his heart.

Blackpool gritted his teeth as his arm was jammed higher behind his back. 'What do you want?'

'Well, I came to see what forensics you have. Listening to your telephone call, where's the bullet?'

'What bullet? What are talking about?'

Vokovic ran the scalpel with a feather touch across Blackpool's throat, leaving smears of crimson hanging to his stubble. 'The next cut goes through the jugular. I won't hesitate to kill you if I don't get the evidence. Are we clear?'

Blackpool felt his legs shaking and breathed heavily. 'OK, It's in the evidence room along the corridor.'

'Which way?'

A sideways nod of the head and Vokovic followed him out of the office, on down the corridor. When they reached the door, Blackpool shouted, 'You'll never get away with this with an APB out. You can have the bullet but you won't get far.'

'Let me worry about that, let's go in. Open the door.'

Blackpool slowly pushed the door wide. Walking in, Sergeant Collins felled Vokovic with one blow of her truncheon across the back of his neck. Collapsing forward, his head banged against the floor, knocking him unconscious. Collins leapt on his back, pulled his arms round and handcuffed him. Blackpool took off his glasses and collapsed onto a chair.

'Cheers'.

Collins smiled. 'Should I still do the debrief?'

31

On the run

August 10th

Diana gripped Blackpool's arm. 'Are you OK after yesterday?'

'I'm fine, thanks to Fiona. She saved my life. The man's handcuffed in the conference room, complaining of a headache. I called Steph; she should be here soon.'

When Steph arrived, they peered in through the room's window.

Diana nodded her head and grunted. 'That's him from the Sauna who tried to kill me. See, there's the tattoo of the Scorpion on his arm. We need him to talk, which won't be easy if he's a trained assassin. Where's the nearest station outside Ingles jurisdiction? Steph, I can't prove it yet, but I think Ingles is involved with whatever the deal is at Sellafield. We can't take any chances.'

'I suggest Morecambe and I know the CID team. I'll take him with two of our PCs.'

Diana grabbed Steph's hands. 'No, I can handle this. I want you to check all the evidence with Blackpool and make sure it's secure. We can't afford to lose that bullet. OK? Get as much background as you can on French, his family and any connections to MI5. I'll drive this man to Morecambe, get him charged and detained. When I'm back, we'll drive to Sellafield to pick up French.'

'Di, that's ridiculous, you can't do this on your own, considering who he is.'

'Steph, I can manage. We'll make sure he's properly handcuffed into one seat and not sitting behind me.'

175

'If you say so. Look, I told you about the flash stick I found at Berwick's house, it's full of equations.'

Before she could carry on, Diana interrupted, 'I've got the same from Faria, she says it's all Berwick's research.'

'If you let me finish. The stick has a covering letter explaining the contents. It has some key equations missing from whatever they have at Sellafield, which I guess is the same on the flash stick Faria gave you. Without those equations the solution won't work.'

'Sly man. Steph, make some copies and I have an idea where they can be kept safely. But now I need to go back to my place, before going to Morecambe.'

Twenty minutes later in her bedroom, she fumbled under the mattress, until her hand grasped cold alloy, her Glock 17 semi-automatic and a box of bullets. She checked the gun over before loading it. The gun fitted into a deep pocket of her parka. Driving back she noticed a black Ford Mondeo in her rear-view mirror. At a fork in the road she took the turning to Waterhead. A minute later she could see the Mondeo two cars back. She turned towards Rothay Bridge before slowing down at the A591 junction. It was still behind. She turned and took the road back to the morgue and called Steph. 'Can you check a reg for me, it's a black Ford Mondeo.'

Steph came back. 'It's a government listed car, nothing more than that.'

'That's either Manners or MI5. They know about our man too I bet.'

Staring out from the front door of the morgue Steph and Diana could see the Mondeo parked nearby.

Steph spoke up. 'Di, I've got an idea on how we can get you out of here.'

Later Steph strode out of the morgue with Blackpool disguised in an overcoat, baseball cap, handcuffed to her and

176

they drove away. The Mondeo followed. The deception lasted until they reached the police station. Emerging from the car, two men blocked their path, flashed their identity cards, and removed Blackpool's hat.

Steph rang Diana. 'I've been tumbled. Where are you?'

'I'm on the road. I managed to sneak our killer out. I thought it would be difficult to get him in my car but surprisingly he didn't resist. Maybe he thinks he can get away on the road. He's not talkative but has an outstanding line in shrugs and sighs. My sat nav shows an hour.'

'Be careful.'

The first twenty minutes were in silence. Wanting to keep MI5 guessing on her final destination Diana took the A592 along the shore of Lake Windermere.

'I'm intrigued, why do they call you The Scorpion? Was it before or after the tattoo. And what happened in Bosnia, that French could get you to kill for him? What did you do wrong?'

He turned and stared out the window and spoke for the first time. 'I shot eight people in the back of the head, executed them in revenge for the murder of my family. It's not like the movies. They don't die instantly. They gurgle blood, exhale, hands shake. There's no capitulation to death, they fight to deny the inevitable. And ever since, I never see a person to kill. They're just targets. The bullet flies and another job is well done. Survival is what matters, so The Scorpion was a perfect name. That answer your question?'

'We were told your name is Emir Vokovic, that right?'

'Yes.'

It was when she turned at the junction of the A590 she picked up another tail. Diana turned right instead of the left to Morecambe, and the car was still behind. Four hundred yards further she did a sudden U turn. Passing the Range Rover. Anyone inside was hidden by tinted windows. She heard a screech of tyres behind, and the SUV sped towards her. She pressed hard on the accelerator.

Nearing Lindale the trailing car arrived faster on her tail, overtook, and slid sideways to a halt in front. Diana slammed on the brakes crashing sideways into the obstacle. Before she could undo her seat belt, a tall, thick set man was at the window pointing a gun, speaking into a phone.

'We've got them, come get me. We're up the road.'

Diana got out of the car, feigning a leg injury. 'Can I sit down?'

'Keys, now.'

Diana handed them over and the man walked past her, round to the rear door, unlocked the seat restraints and yanked Vokovic out. Diana leapt upwards and pressed her Glock into the back of the man's head, shouting at Vokovic.

'Behind me! If you go with these guys, that's curtains. You're a loose end.'

To her surprise he came. Diana pressed the muzzle harder into the back of the skull.

'Give me my keys back.' Diana took the keys and unlocked the boot, 'Get in.'

Diana shut the boot, locked the crashed car, and tossed the keys away. She stared at Vokovic. 'How did they discover we were here?'

'Tracking on your phone, or maybe hidden a device in your car.

'He's already phoned for back up and they'll be here soon. Stay on the roads and we will be caught. There's an alternative they might not consider, but not my first choice. We need to get to Grange Over Sands.'

She used her phone one last time on Google Maps to double check. It was a walk she'd done a few time before. She threw the phone away and got into the Range Rover. It took several key presses before the engine growled into life. She drove the battered car along the Windermere road down into Grange Over

Sands. Tourists spilled out of the coffee shops onto the windy street, startled by the sudden screech of bumper dragging over the tarmac. A sharp downward turn ended on the bayfront car park. Diana dropped the keys into a waste bin. A few minutes later they were on the promenade, a concrete curved walkway for a mile in each direction.

Vokovic asked, 'What's the plan?'

Diana pointed to the far shore, beyond a wide expanse of nothing except greying sand and the sea way in the distance. The infamous Morecambe Sands.

Diana walked on with Vokovic trailing behind, fighting off the pain of a damaged leg, blood soaking into his jeans. Minutes later Vokovic shouted ahead.

'I'm struggling. Ahead there's a station, let's catch a train.'

'Don't be daft. We are on the run; they will check all trains. Trust me. We get to the end of this path and walk onto that land sticking out, Holme Island. It's a half an hour walk maybe across the sands to Park Point. We can walk down into Silverdale and get a car down to Morecambe.'

'Why Morecambe?'

'It's not the Lakes.'

They trudged twenty minutes into the treacherous expanse, leaving a trail of footprints in the damp sands, under the darkening grey as the sun fell lower in the sky in front of them. In the far distance the lights of Morecambe were coming on and upstream fog was rolling over the sands.

They carried on in silence for another five minutes, before Vokovic shouted out. 'This is like walking through mud. Every step is an effort and are these handcuffs necessary?'

Diana turned and waved the automatic at him. 'If we don't hurry wet sand won't be the problem, we'll be swimming against the incoming tide. Keep walking behind and follow my footsteps. There's difficult to spot quicksand pools. Loads of people have died out here, sucked in or caught by the tide that catches you before you can get away. Horses, tractors, trailers, and a van have sunk in, never recovered. Stick with me if you want to survive, like the fells it might look picturesque, but it can be deadly.'

'You're not local, how come you know so much about this place. You're crazy, you'll get us both killed.'

'I used to come here when I was young with my Dad and I've walked it twice recently. Look, if we stayed at Grange or anywhere on the road, they would find us and you will be dead. I told you, you are a loose end that needs tidying up, I am too.'

Vokovic turned back. 'I need to take my shoes off, sands getting in.'

'Make it quick.'

The man bent down slid off a trainer and standing on one leg, he shook out the sand. 'Tell me how far is it?'

'If we speed up, we should get across in half an hour and not get caught in the incoming tide.'

He switched to the foot. 'Tell me, what do you get out of this?'

'Justice.'

'You are naïve.'

Vokovic took a few steps forward, calling behind Diana's back. 'You do know you are never going to shoot me.'

He walked around her and moved in until Diana's gun muzzle was right against his chest and spat out each word.

'Never.... Gonna.... happen.'

He gripped the muzzle, pushing it downwards. Diana's hands were shaking.

'I'm a trained killer, trained by specialists. I've killed from a distance, face to face, with guns, with knives, with my bare hands.'

He stood back, there was no emotion just a hard-unblinking stare. 'Detective, you're not a killer. I've stared into the eyes of people waving guns and it's not in you. It's OK on a practice range but this is different, cold blooded, in front of you, staring into my eyes, having to watch the life ebb out of me.'

Diana was trying her upmost to ignore the darts of conscience as she put her arm out at full length and pointed the automatic with her finger on the trigger. 'Who hired you?'

'Your arm is shaking. It's not like anything you have ever faced and against your rules. This is cold and calculated. You've never faced this in the field have you? I bet you're not aware but there's sweat on your face.'

Vokovic squatted on his haunches, running the sand through his fingertips.

'But that's not true. You have faced this before. I know what happened to you in February. The report reads you caught up with the terrorist as he was about to go into the arena and shot him. See to me, that doesn't ring true, because the bomb still went off. Aren't police trained to shoot at the head to stop a terrorist pressing that button. So I'm guessing you didn't shoot till it was too late. In my experience torments are either faced full on or allowed to corrode the soul. First, it's your thoughts affected, memories and emotions follow, till all your behaviour is infected. Except in this case I'll bet it's your faith too. Diana Petrou the Christian copper. You've hung on to the idiocy of believing in a God. You believe shooting me would be a mortal sin, condemn you to hell?'

'Shut up about that, my faith has nothing to do with this. Tell me the truth about these killings and we can see what deal can be done. You have murdered two maybe three people and you are in the middle of a conspiracy. I'm not giving up till we get justice.'

'You shot; however the bomb still went off. Conscience made you hesitate. Has your faith told you to feel guilty for those who died in the blast? They call you a hero because you saved those in the stadium. I've seen first-hand the evil, the corruption, the hypocrisy of the world that can make human life worthless. You believe in God that lays on you the need to practice kindness. It makes you weak and vulnerable then Srebrenica happens.'

'Shut up! Tell me what you did and who ordered you to do it.'

Distracted, in one painful, sharp action The Scorpion chopped Diana's legs away with one swing of his right leg. As she fell, he grabbed the gun from her hand. She ended flat on her back in the wet sand. He towered over her with one demand.

'Key!'

The handcuffs dropped onto Diana's chest. 'You are pathetic. Let me tell what this world is like. Have a look around you at, the colours, the beauty, the smells, the majesty of those fells in the distance. It's all rubbish. If you delve under the surface, it's a brutal vicious world where animals are killing and devouring one another alive.'

Diana was paralysed with fear, feeling no doubt she was the next victim, but he carried on.

'What God concocts this violent world? God does not exist! We are the evolutionary product of a dog-eat-dog world, the survival of the fittest and we do what's expected to be the fittest. I have some advice for you to survive, ditch God and your guilt will go away. There is no God. I'll tell you again, compassion and kindness makes you weak and vulnerable.'

Diana closed her eyes and prayed out loud. There was a sound of fading footsteps. She looked up. Vokovic was striding off into the twilight. Diana shouted from desperation into the air. Vokovic, turned shaking his head, laughing. Diana laid back in the sand, calming herself, watching the clouds darkening above. It was minutes before she sat up and decided to give chase, but the path still needed caution. The figure in the distance had disappeared into the greying twilight.

It was twenty minutes later she heard a faint cry. She quickened her pace. When she reached Vokovic, he was caught in quicksand pleading to be pulled out. Diana knelt down, shaking her head. 'I told you there was quicksand here. Don't struggle, you'll sink deeper. I'll pull you out, after you answer my question.'

Pointing the Glock. 'Pull me out!'

'Well shooting me won't help you, we both die. Besides, you might notice the tide beginning to come in too. It will take about maybe twenty or thirty minutes to get here. This is a onetime offer. You are either going to sink further in and suffocate or drown in the incoming tide. That happens fast and I'm not hanging around to watch you die. Tell me who hired you and I will pull you out.'

'If I tell you what I know they will kill you. This is much bigger that you think.'

'I don't care. Stay here, you will die. Tell me. Maybe I will give you the chance to get away.'

Vokovic, shifted and sank a little further. 'OK, it's Mark, Mark French.'

'Why did he have people killed?'

'It's tied up with the other guy I killed, Berwick Stewart, a discovery he made. Mark, I think, is set to make a fortune.'

'How did you know about Givens and Wilson? Why have them killed?

'I don't know, I never want to know, I just do my job. Now, for heaven's sake, drag me out.'

Diana started to walk away before Vokovic shouted. 'Faria. Talk to Faria, she knows more than anyone.'

Diana turned back, took off her jacket, laid out on the sand and flung one arm towards him. After three attempts he managed to grab one of the sleeves. Diana pulled hard. Nothing happened till the stiches unravelled one at a time, the sleeve snapped away, he sank further.

'C'mon. Help me!'

'Alright, grab this.'

Diana slid a little further forward to throw the other sleeve. Vokovic grabbed it. In his urgency he sank up to his waist, legs held fast. Diana could see the tide begin to flow over the sandy surface in the distance. Vokovic grasped the sleeve with two hands. Diana pulled as hard as she could, but he was stuck fast.

Diana caught her breath. 'See if your legs can move at all.'

Diana flung the sleeve once again and pulled, straining hard, nothing happened. The stitching began to unravel.

Diana looked behind. The tide was coming nearer. 'Come on one last try.'

Vokovic shook her head.

'No point both of us dying.'

'No. I'm not leaving here without you. I'm not letting you die.'

Diana took off her sweatshirt, knotted the arms to the sleeves of the jacket and threw the coat. Vokovic grabbed hold and Diana pulled with all her strength. Vokovic felt his legs shift. Looking behind the tide was only a few minutes away. Only then did the coat rip apart and Diana collapse back on the sand.

There was a moment silence before Vokovic spoke. 'There's no point both of us dying.'

Diana crawled forward and reached out. 'Grab my hands.' Then she pulled with all her strength, eyes closed, shouting out through gritted teeth. Vokovic let go. 'I'm not moving, I'm stuck.'

'I'm really sorry, this is all my fault.'

'No recriminations. My life, my choices.'

Diana stood. 'I'm so sorry. Any last wishes?'

'My sister's name is Amina. She lives in Siena. Please get a message to her, tell her what happened. Tell her I loved her and the children, so much.'

'I promise.'

Diana mouthed her regrets, stood, but turned back. 'Lord, please forgive this man,' then ran. Needing to beat the tide and she ran faster, her lungs burning. A minute later she heard a single gunshot.

32

Badlands

Aug 11th

All the Google entries that Mark searched were about Petrou's heroics at the bombing. The woman who was a nuisance before, was in danger of stumbling into what was really happening. Intent on his laptop, he only noticed Neil Denver when he threw a newspaper onto his keyboard.

'I didn't sanction this.'

The headline ran, *Police search for a serial killer after death of Gabriel Wood.* Mark tossed the paper aside. 'Nothing to do with me. It's what it says, they have a serial killer.'

'Bullshit. I've seen the autopsy reports, three expert sniper kills. Smacks of your friend The Scorpion. Yesterday, the resident pathologist requested a database search at MOD from a fingerprint. He found the name of a Bosnian who served in your unit, Emir Vokovic, who I presume is The Scorpion. He's responsible for shooting these people, on your orders I presume. Why?'

Mark got up and took a bottle from a drawer to pour them both a whisky. 'I caught Kim Givens in my office going through my laptop with her phone in her hand. The page she was looking at wasn't enough to tell her exactly what we are planning, but enough to tell her it was something secret. I arranged surveillance on her phone. She mailed a screenshot to the builder Adam Wilson. Maybe she thought that Adam was involved in the construction and didn't realise how secret it was. The mail she photo'd was from Anne, making it crystal clear that this was led by the Government. There were two people who could leak that and jeopardise all of our plans. So I sorted the problem.

'What happened to the images.'

Mark threw over a phone. 'We found Adam Wilson's phone on his boat before the police arrived and took his laptop too. There was no trace of him sending this to anyone else. I decided to deal with this in a way that doesn't come back to us. It's worked. After the third random killing they have been chasing their tails thinking it's either a serial killer or a hired killer by our local drug kingpin, Dan Jetty.'

'You should have talked to me. I sanctioned Berwick Stewart, which was necessary. He was going to blow it all for the government. Lucky for us your sniper is dead. He tried to cross Morecambe Bay yesterday. I guess he thought he wouldn't be followed. Looks like he got caught in quicksand, shot himself before drowning. We know Petrou was with him. A walker on the sands found him this morning still stuck. I've spoken to Ingles; he's going to maintain the fraudulent claim that they have found their serial killer. He'll get his promised payment. Leave DCI Petrou and DC Giles to me. Don't go near them.'

Mark lied. 'No plans to go near them. Where is Berwick's research?'

'There's only three people with copies; you, me and the Minister. This will make the government enough income to offset all its debt. Our Minister will be in line, if we succeed, to be the next PM, showing gratitude to the security services. You'll be set for life too.'

Eyes blinking, lying on a cold stone floor, Diana stared at a single light bulb in the ceiling. Her head was throbbing, her memory returning. The memories were hazy of getting across the sands just before the tide hit, then walking, trying towards Silverdale train station. There was a car behind. What next? Two men emerged grabbing her. A jab in the arm.

She stood up, tried the door, it was locked. Footsteps were coming, a shout of, 'Stand back,' and Neil Denver walked in carrying a wooden chair.

'Sit down. How are you, Diana? You couldn't leave things alone. I warned you. The CCTV from the bombing is on the way to the press and the inquest.'

'Beat you to it Neil. I've written to the inquest with the full confession.'

'Oh the honest copper admitting her responsibility at last but let's face it, you are finished. We'll lock you up here whilst deciding what to do with you to keep you from interfering.'

'How did you know where I was?'

'We planted trackers on The Scorpion's belt. That's his trade name by the way, appropriate for his deadly skills.'

'I've seen his tattoo.'

'When we realised the idiotic thing you were doing, trying to cross Morecambe Sands, we arranged a greeting party.'

Diana went to stand up before Neil pulled out a gun. She sat back on the chair. 'What happened to The Scorpion? How come he got caught in quicksand? Someone found him this morning, shot.

'He got my gun and ran off. I found him later and tried to get him out but he was too stuck. I walked away and heard the gunshot behind me.'

Neil grabbed Diana's throat, 'What did he tell you?'

'Nothing. Tell me what's going on?'

'You go first.'

Diana grinned. 'Well it's not a serial killer or Jetty. We have a trained sniper, who was with Mark French in Bosnia. Could French have persuaded him to kill three people? And what's the reason Kim Givens and Adam Wilson needed to die? He used the same bullets and the same gun but left a fingerprint on the bullet which killed Gabriel Wood. I'm guessing Gabriel was an innocent victim trying to persuade us it was a serial killer, poor sod. If French ordered them killed, I'm guessing Berwick Stewart needed to be killed too. Now you have me locked up here. So why kill all these people?'

Neil turned back to the door. 'It's original research that Berwick did. The government owns it but he was going to share it with the world, which we couldn't let happen. Give Berwick his due, his endeavours went beyond the limit of our expectations, but he kept going and made a breakthrough. It's game changing for the worlds' energy supply. We will have complete control of its sale. The UK Government, and will retain all the revenue from it, and that's all I'm saying. You will have to be our guest for a few days until we can announce it. We'll find you a better room.'

'Always comes down to money doesn't it. You tell me all that and am I getting out here alive?'

Neil only shrugged his shoulders. 'Your Super, Ingles, has been working with us, he's telling your colleagues you have gone missing and is disseminating all the proof that Jetty hired Vokovic. He was a gun for hire. He and Jetty were talking for months, we intercepted their phone calls. Thanks to you we have Cody giving verification on why Jetty had a reason for them both to disposed of. For Stewart, we have his wife arrested on suspicion. It's all tying up nicely. You don't get me, do you? Maybe you think I'm a well-bred, civil servant. I grew up in Battersea before it was gentrified, when it was tough and full of gangs. I educated my way out, but without losing a ruthless streak, I'll do whatever is needed to complete my task. If we let you out, you'll have to go along with all this. How likely is that? Here's water.'

Neil handed over a plastic bottle. Diana handed it back.

'Oh, you are suspicious.'

Neil took a gulp, offered it back, picked up the chair and left. The door slammed shut, Diana thought, I'm never getting out of here.

The sound of boots on the stone floor grew louder. Diana felt into her trouser pockets, realising they left a pen in her pocket. She worked the nib against the stone floor

She lay down on the floor with her hands under her body. A voice at the door shouted out. 'Back against the wall!'

The guard entered and Diana lay still on the floor.

'Get up!'

Diana was motionless. The guard laid down the food tray, leaned over Diana who plunged the pen nib into the guard's neck. He fell backwards screaming in pain. She ran out into a starkly lit corridor. To the right, some ten yards away, she saw the stairs.

Behind her the guard was shouting. 'She's out!'

Diana stood still on the fifth step as a man ran below towards the cell. Diana leapt upwards two steps at a time. On reaching the third flight, she heard the alarm raised, voices shouting.

Four more flights, the stairs came to an end. She pushed at a metal door and found herself on the roof. There was a foot-wide narrow path on the apex of an 'A' frame. She gingerly stepped out saying to herself, 'Don't panic,' as she looked down. Her legs shook and her palms sweated. She shuffled forward with feet crossing over to stay as safe as possible. She stood still when men came out into the courtyard, guns over their shoulders. A few yards ahead was a chimney. She took the chance and ran. Reaching the chimney, her foot slipped off the pathway. She pulled herself up, clinging to the chimney but her foot shifted a loose slat downwards. The slate garnered momentum caught the guttering and halted.

Diana breathed again, hiding on the other side of the chimney. The six men below were heading off in different directions with shouts of, 'Find her!'

Ahead the roof path ended with a gap into an adjacent flat roof with little room for a run up. The gap disappeared into darkness. Diana took several steps backwards and leapt. She landed on the gravelled roof, legs dangling over the edge.

Diana clawed at the gravel until her feet made it onto the floor of the roof. She ran towards a far door. Minutes later, she was down the flights of stairs and cowering behind a door on the ground floor. She opened it a crack and peered into an alleyway. About to run out, a figure appeared carrying a gun. Pulling the door closed she held her breath till the footsteps walked away. She ran out, along alleyways emerging, to her surprise, into Kirkfields. She'd been in Ambleside the whole time.

33

Exit music

August 12th

Speeding out of Ambleside on the Great Langdale road, Diana and Steph sat in silence, realising what they were about to do might finish both their careers. The turning towards Wrynose Pass took them onto a single-track road and the rain was getting heavier.

'Steph, you didn't have to do this, but thank you for driving, you are better on the passes at night. You are the only person I can trust.'

'It's OK, I'm with you on this.'

'Did you bring the gun?'

'Glove compartment, it's another Glock 17 from the evidence room. Di, I found out what they are hiding. On that flash stick I found at Berwick's, in one memo it makes it evident he cracked the problem of how waste radioactive fuel can be completely and safely recycled.'

Diana exclaimed. 'What!'

'His memo says he wanted this made available to the whole world. Is it that important?'

Diana let out an audible gasp. 'Too right it is. Don't you get it?'

'Before we get into that, what are we going to do when we get to Sellafield?'

'Arrest French and take him to my old nick, where we can trust people to question and charge him. What happens after that, I'm not sure. Come on let's drive on.'

'I have this flash stick with me. Can you take it?'

At the head of the valley they were enclosed on all sides by the dark looming fells. They began to climb the hair pinned road of Wrynose Pass, the steepest road in Britain. It was pitch black, with the syncopated sounds of heavy raindrops on the car roof. As Steph dropped to second gear, they both shared an unspoken foreboding.

'Steph, can you pull over. I need to tell you about the bombing before we get to Sellafield. I've tried to live up to the idea that evil happens when good people do nothing. That's where we are at right now.'

'OK, but it's pouring down, a few more turns and we can rest at the summit. Then you can tell me about the bombing. OK? The descent in this rain won't be easy.'

'No, please pull in now, I need you to hear this.'

Fifty yards on Steph pulled up on a grass verge. 'Di, what is it that's so important?'

Diana turned to face Steph. 'I've told this to my husband and now made it public. When I faced Affredi I didn't shoot him. I hesitated. I've never killed anyone before. I told him to get on his knees but he set off the bomb. Because of me many people died and were maimed but I let the story be told that I did try to kill him.'

Steph gripped the steering wheel hard looking directly ahead and said nothing for a minute. 'I haven't killed anyone either, so can't tell you if I would have acted differently.'

Diana went to say something but Steph held up her hand to stop her. 'You didn't set off a bomb and kill people. He made that choice. But I understand why you feel guilty for lying about it. You are the most decent person I've worked with. So what happens now?'

'Now it's out there, it will be the end of my career.'

Steph turned. 'Maybe it won't be if we can arrest French and solve these murders.

The wipers were struggling to keep up. Rounding the last bend to the summit, Steph slammed her foot on the brakes and the seatbelts bit into their chests. The car slid sideways inches away from an SUV parked across the road. Diana was about to say, 'You OK?' when a tall, hooded figure emerged. Before they could react, he raised a gun and shot.

Diana shouted, 'Duck!'

It was too late. He aimed at Steph. The first shot missed its target, the second hit her shoulder. Steph screamed out in pain. Diana rolled out onto the road and shot. It missed, letting the man jump back into the SUV and drive away.

Back in the car, blood was oozing from Steph's shoulder. Diana grabbed Steph's right hand, 'Press hard. I'll get help.'

'Di, it's OK, the bullet just grazed me, it's not in me.'

She kept repeating'm OK as the blood ran down her arm. Diana ran out into the rain, searching for a signal and dialled.

'This is DCI Petrou; can you hear me?'

She screamed at the top of her voice. 'This is DCI Petrou; we are at the summit of Wrynose. We've been shot at but the shooter's got away, I want back up here now.

Back in the car, Steph had torn off part of T Shirt and wrapped it around her arm.

'It looks OK Steph, but still want you to go to hospital to check it and get it properly bandaged.'

Diana kicked Ingles door hard, walking in, pointing the automatic straight at his head.

'You bastard, you thought I was driving to Sellafield last night. You didn't count on Steph driving, did you?'

Ingles rose from his chair, 'Put the gun down, this is your career finished Petrou. Collins get in here!'

Before Collins could enter, Diana jammed a chair under the door handle. 'No-one's coming in till I get answers.'

Ingles started to walk around the desk, 'Put the gun down, you are making a massive mistake.'

'Sit down!'

Ingles backed away, both hands raised, palms up. 'OK, OK, I didn't tell anyone where you were going. Did Steph tell anyone? Did anyone follow you? You probably didn't bother to see. What reason do I have to harm you?'

Diana advanced, arm outstretched, the Glock 17 pointed at Ingles head. 'You callous sod. Someone tried to kill your DC and that's all down to you. The conversation with the Scorpion was revealing, he confessed to shooting Givens and Wilson also murdering Stewart, all paid for by his Army buddy French. I'm getting the sense that French is doing a deal for a substantial reward. You and our Minister Anne Manners are all involved.

'Diana, put the gun down. You won't shoot me and you are talking nonsense. I'm not involved with any murders.'

Diana pulled out her iPhone, pressed play on her recordings. Faria's voice sang out.

'Ingles is in it up to his neck. He's used his position to guarantee that the investigations were deflected, for a fee. He's getting a slice of the deal.'

Diana hit pause. 'The Scorpion's name was Vokovic, a sniper who served under Mark French in Bosnia. He told me loads before he died. I've sent this to my former Super, with instructions on what to do if I go missing or turn up dead. I reckon you have two options. Either you confess and ask for a deal, if in return you rat out the others involved, or go on the run. I'm going to arrest French. This ends today.'

'Diana, wait, let me explain.'

Diana leaned over the desk. 'Shut up. If we get the proof you set up Steph being shot, that's attempted murder.'

Striding into North Street, she stuffed the Glock into the belt of her jeans. Steph's phone was still in her pocket. She rang Sellafield. French's new PA told her he was going walking on his favourite fell, Blencathra. He drove off about an hour ago. She ran to the taxi rank.

'Take me to Threlkeld.'

In the back of the cab, she was thinking what to do when she confronted French. With luck she'd get ahead of French on the fell. She knew Ingles would warn French she was coming. What was the deal that was going down? With Anne Manners involved this might be a huge political scandal. MI5 were involved too, who else in the government knew?

34

Bodysnatchers

August 13th

Without sunlight on its southern expanse, Blencathra was threatening, desolate, isolated. Diana stared at the three ridges, rising like jagged fingers pointing to the summit of an unknown fate. She remembered a quote that dangers retreat when boldly confronted. The landlord of the pub told her that the quickest way to the summit, was not over the precarious ridges, but a straightforward, clear path a mile up the road above Scales Farm. She set off, pulling on her green fleece, checking the semi-automatic in a deep pocket.

The initial path was a wide gravel track and soon struck a quick rhythm. Afterwards there was a path at a constant forty-five degrees across the side of the first ascent. It took twenty minutes before she caught sight of Mark French maybe ten minutes ahead. She checked Steph's phone still had a signal and made a call. Sergeant Collins answered.

'Collins, I'm walking up Blencathra, chasing Mark French. Can you organise back-up. I need some officers following me up the fell and some waiting in Threlkeld in case he gets away from me.'

'Ma'am, you should wait for back-up. Chasing him up there alone is reckless.'

Diana answered, 'I'll be fine.' and switched off the phone.

No one else was in sight ahead or behind. She zipped up her fleece and quickened her pace. The blue sky was disappearing behind creeping dark clouds. Half an hour later she rounded the crest and ran across grassy level ground with the summit in plain sight, until she reached Scales Tarn. Ahead French was sitting by the water. The surface was still, a black reflection of Diana's first sight of Sharp Edge. It appeared to be a thin, perilous ridge that ran upwards towards the summit, above a rockface of stones, gravel, heather, and grass.

French was taking a drink from his backpack. Ripples were starting to creep across the tarn from light raindrops. He pulled out a yellow cagoule, stood and peered backwards. Diana ducked down. French started his ascent of a curved, rocky path that led to the beginning of the Edge above. They were alone. Diana followed, keeping a safe distance, fearful of what she was about to encounter, hoping French wouldn't recognise her. The rain turned into a steady drizzle and ahead French had disappeared.

Five minutes later, Diana reached the ridge and there was French sitting on a rock, waiting for her.

'You caught me up at last. You will enjoy this,' pointing to the rocky path of Sharp Edge, 'Watch your step in the rain.'

French walked out onto the narrow Edge. Diana felt the first flushes of anxiety; palms sweating, mouth drying and arms shaking. The path was just random rocky pinnacles to negotiate with sharp tops rising upwards, all now wet. Either side were the perilous sheer slopes, hundreds of feet downwards. She remembered the state of Berwick Stewart's body. Stepping a few feet further, the whole panorama started to spin. Nausea rose in her throat and sweat soaked her shirt. She sat down again, gripping the rocks either side, shutting her eyes. French turned with a satisfied grin. 'Having a panic attack? It's not too late to go back. See you.'

Diana lifted herself up on one elbow to watch a swaying figure in the distance. She took her gun out and shot in the air shouting, 'Come back! You are under arrest.'

French walked back, leaning over her prone figure. 'What am I under arrest for?'

'Conspiracy to murder Kim Givens, Adam Wilson, Berwick Stewart, Gabriel Wood, and the attempted murder of DC Stephanie Giles.'

'Interesting, how are you going to arrest me? Your hand's shaking. You frightened

French gripped Diana's wrist. Laughing, he took the automatic from Diana's hand.

'Glock 17 semi-automatic, decent weapon. Should I shoot you and roll you over the side?'

Diana didn't dare look up. French pushed the muzzle against the side of her head.

'Look at me! I learnt a secret about you DCI Petrou, Neil showed me the CCTV footage.'

'What secret?'

'The CCTV shows you had a moment when you could have shot him before he could set the bomb off. You didn't shoot until it was too late.'

French sat down. 'What prevented you? I'm guessing you have never killed anyone before. It's against your faith to kill in cold blood. Is that it?'

Diana finally turned, and bravely poked French in the chest. 'I can live with what I've done, can you?'

French stood again laughing. 'No problem. Unlike you I get the job done. You lacked the courage to do the right thing, to kill a terrorist and save lives. But worse you let everyone think you were a hero.'

Diana stood up. 'My confession is out with the press and the inquest. I can't be blackmailed anymore and this will be my last arrest as a copper.'

French squared up to Diana. 'Really. I'm surprised. See, I'm with Machiavelli, the ends do justify the means. By the way what happened to the Scorpion? Neil tells me he's dead.'

Diana sat up. 'He got caught in quicksand in Morecambe Bay, shot himself before drowning.'

'Not before he told all I bet. Fitting way to go. He never got over Bosnia but became a great killer for hire.'

Diana asked. 'Tell me, what's this all about, what makes killing these people worthwhile?'

'You want to know. OK. Answer this my DCI. What's our planet's most urgent challenge?'

Diana answered, playing for time, looking for a moment. 'I dunno, climate change I suppose.'

French shook his head. 'Population. We'll be ten billion soon. All those people devour energy, that's more, oil, gas and coal all driving the climate change. We need, a non-polluting alternative on an enormous scale. Berwick Stewart did original research. He discovered how we could safely recycle all the waste generated in a nuclear plant. Are you listening?'

Diana stopped shifting around. 'Yes, go on.'

'It's the most dangerous waste and expensive to dispose of safely. Berwick's research alters all that. Nuclear becomes the preferred energy source, without pollution and one that produces enormous energy, efficiently, more than any of the other renewables. The Government makes billions selling the solution to other countries and shares revenue with the Chinese building Power Stations globally.'

Keeping French talking, Diana's thoughts were more focused on weighing up the options to get out of this. She struggled for another question. 'So why kill Stewart?'

'Berwick was an idealist and planned to share this with the whole world for free. We couldn't let that happen.'

French seemed in his element, standing, waving the Glock to make a point, holding forth, arms flung wide. 'We wipe out this country's debt. I get rich for managing all this, MI5 get a potential Prime Minister who is in their debt.'

Diana pointed up the Edge.

'Someone's coming.'

In the moment French turned, Diana leapt forward and knocked him over. She fell on top of him bashing his hand against a craggy rock which pierced his skin and the gun dropped. Diana smashed her fist into his cheek but French threw her off and they both rolled free. Standing, they ran at each other.

199

Their hands clasped in a trial of strength until French's foot slipped on a wet rock and they both tumbled off rolling .

Diana halted her slide by grasping a rocky outgrowth. French slid down beside her, stopping himself by grasping Diana's foot. Diana was back in the Stadium, staring at Michael Affredi. A moment of possible redemption. Diana looked down at the man below pleading for help. French slid further down, grabbing at one rock to come to a halt. Diana could see he was clinging on by his fingertips. French cried out.

'Help me!'

Diana stared into the frightened eyes, doing nothing. He didn't deserve to live, until something inside made her act. Lying on her back she slid slowly further down, finding rocks to press against with her feet. French swung his free hand and grabbed Diana's trousers but one by one his fingers came loose. Diana eased off her fleece and threw the coat sleeves towards French, who grabbed onto the long arms. Diana prayed for the stitching to hold and he pulled. She was back on Morecambe sands. French was hanging on, pulling himself upwards, boots clawing for any foothold, until he lay beside her.

Diana crawled upwards, back onto the edge, picking up the Glock. French followed behind, lying flat on the ground, he grinned up at Diana, 'Why are you bothering, you won't shoot me.'

Diana, stood, grinned back, and shot him in the leg. French yelped and swore. Diana dialled a number. 'That will stop you getting away. Is that you Collins? I need back up on Sharp Edge. I've arrested Mark French for conspiracy to murder. He's a bit cut up; send a medic too. Where's the Super?'

'Ma'am, Ingles went off earlier and didn't tell anyone where he was going. And Giles is fine, they've patched her up.'

'Collins, Ingles is part of this. Get an APB out on him under my authority. Tell them to hurry, I'm getting soaked up here.'

French pulled off a shirt and wrapped it around his leg. 'You bitch.'

They sat in silence till French said. 'This changes nothing. I've got the 'get out of jail free' cards and our dear friend Neil Denver has too. Nothing is going to prevent us using Berwick's research.'

Diana said nothing. She put her fleece back on, unzipped the inside pocket and gripped the flash stick. 'If you say so.'

35

Live and let live.

August 16th

Neil was sitting in Ingles chair, sipping coffee when Martins came in. He offered a handshake across the desk.

'DC Martins, pleased to meet you. I'm Neil Denver; you may have heard my name mentioned.'

'Sure, the MI5 man.'

'Sit down. Let me bring you up to date. Superintendent Ingles has retired. DCI Petrou is under suspicion of attempted murder. DC Giles is on bail for aiding and abetting. That leaves you in charge for the moment. I presume you are happy to manage the place?'

Martins blinked, taciturn.

Neil paraded around the desk, gripping Martin's shoulder from behind. 'I'll take that to be a yes. Onto other matters. You have in custody Mark French. The tale spun by your DCI is false. She tried to murder Mr French out of revenge in the mistaken belief that Mr French shot at DC Giles. It was all part of ridiculous conspiracy theories about Sellafield. It is now determined that the three murders on lake Windermere were ordered Dan Jetty who hired a killer, John Castle. Conclude that investigation and release Mr French.'

Martins gripped on to the arms of the chair. 'I am sorry but all of that doesn't sound right to me. We have a lack forensic proof on John Castle and his suicide note reads he didn't do it.'

'I think you will find we have no suicide note. Am I making myself understood?

'But we do have other information on a potential killer. Until all this is resolved I don't think I should release Mr French.'

Neil swung Martin's chair around and spat out. 'OK, let me put it this way. DC Martins you will do as you are told, otherwise your little arrangement with Dan Jetty will be made public, for which you can be charged and will go to prison. You understand?'

Martins stared in fear as the grip on his arm got tighter. 'Um, eh…...whatever you say. I'll go get Mr French.'

Steph opened her front door. 'So you are discharged.'

'Hi Di. Yes, I was lucky, no major damage. Got to keep a bandage on that's all. Collins tells me you arrested French.'

'I did, but MI5 have already got him released. The cover up begins. I wanted to say something to you. I never expected to find a true friendship with a colleague. We cracked this case as a partnership. Trouble is, will anyone get convicted? From what I've confessed about the bombing and lying to an inquest, I won't be a policewoman anymore.'

'It's not right Di, there must be something we can do. Let's go get a coffee.'

The café was surprisingly quiet. Sitting in the shade, in the quiet, after the traumas of the night before. Diana and Steph were both swiping the chocolate off the surface of their Cappuccinos. Diana looked up 'Berwick's discovery is a game changer but our government is only interested in making immense revenues from it. I can finish what he set out to do. Let the world know about his discovery for free and use it.'

Steph thought for a moment. 'Sorry, isn't that a little above our pay grade? We are just provincial coppers and you are talking about taking on the government.'

'I know, it seems that way, but this is my chance to do something worthwhile. We have the flash stick, which means only we have the full solution Berwick worked out. They still don't know that and that we have it. He could see the value of letting the world know, not keeping it for profit. I can do some good.'

Steph leaned across the table and held Diana's hand. 'Di, as a friend, I have to say, are you not just trying to make up for what happened at the bombing. What's the word? To get some atonement?'

'Maybe, but that doesn't stop this being the right thing to do. I mean we could just hand over the flash stick. The government wins out but what will they do with me. I know French arranged for four murders but they can't let that come out. Denver blackmailed me and I have the confession Vokovic made to me. Haven't they shown how ruthless they are. They believe the ends justifies the means'

Steph sat back in her chair. 'What about me?'

'I don't know. I was the one with Vokovic when he died, I'm the one who arrested French and Denver has already tried to lock me up. So you might be OK.'

'Di, I hate the word might. We are still a partnership, tell me what your plan is.'

Diana looked around to make sure they weren't overheard. 'Alright, here's my plan. I've gone low tech and printed out a hard copy of the complete research, including the missing portion. I've hidden it in the evidence box about John Castle.'

Step interrupted. 'Why hard copy?'

'Hard copy, non-electronic, is the only way to distribute this and give it a chance to reach its targets. Anything electronic can be tracked, traced, shut down. So I want to get hundreds of copies made from my printout then leave that original where it is and wait for a contact of mine, Wiley, to be in touch. Wiley's his nickname, an ex-con who specialises in forgery. He was a snitch for me for years. He's the single person I can trust not to talk to the authorities, to do what has to be done.'

'What will you do with the copies?'

'Wiley will get a group of, shall we call them colleagues, together and pay them a couple grand each to deliver these printed copies to scientists, journalists and activists, around the UK.'

Steph grabbed Diana's hand again 'Let me get the copies done. You can't go anywhere near Keswick station; they will arrest you.

'That makes sense but please be careful, I'd like to keep you out of danger.'

'I will. What's your plan after that?'

'The only place I can think to go to, to hide away is back to my father's home, Santorini. I know that sounds crazy, it's so far away, but I can hide out there hopefully for long enough whilst Wiley does his thing. Trouble is getting there. If I fly, I'm sure they will pick me up at the airport. I need to find another way.'

Steph rang Martine to persuaded her to go to her family for safety, then took a cab, rather than her own car, up to Keswick.

She used Diana's security badge, to get into the building and found the printed copy in Castle's box in the evidence room. She sat in an unoccupied corner by the photocopier. Her plan was to put the original back and take a copy to a local printer she knew. She loaded up the report, over eighty pages long, into the photocopier, pushed start and waited.

It was five minutes later that Neil Denver strode into the office with Martins in tow. Steph crept over and pushed pause on the photocopier. Denver was screaming at Martins that Petrou's badge was used, and she must be in the building. In scrambling to hide under a desk a stapler fell onto the floor. Martins was still busy going through the security log when Neil followed the noise.

One step away, about to bend down to pick up the stapler, Martins called out, 'I'm looking at the log on my phone, she used her badge to get into the evidence room, only five minutes ago.'

'Well she hasn't come past us. Put out another APB. She can't have got far. Are there any other routes out of this building?'

'Only other exit is onto the roof and there's a fire escape up there.'

With that they ran off. Steph crawled out. The next minutes were agonising viewing the numbers counting down. The last sheet emerged; the complete solution was printed out. She heard voices coming down the stairs from the roof and crouched back under the desk. Going back to the evidence room wasn't an option, it would show the use of the badge. She could only wait, eyes shut, breathing heavily, praying they would leave.

It was another five agonising minutes before Neil reappeared shouting at Martins. 'She's got away, it's your fault, get out, get her found.'

Martins departed; Neil made a call. Thirty minutes later Steph was back in her flat with the printouts in her holdall.

'I didn't expect to be back here.'

Neil sat, taping the table with his fingers, adjusting his tie. 'Sit down, you fool. Let's see how we can clear up the mess you've made. The slip ups must end or you are history. You are only going to do what we tell you to do nothing more, nothing less.'

Mark French nodded. Neil stood up. 'There's a Japanese proverb. The nail sticking up has to be hammered down. But we have more than one nail because of your actions. So, this is what's going to happen. The Scorpion's death we can put on Petrou if that's necessary and the attempt on your life. We will plant bits of evidence to show John Castle was responsible for the killings on Windermere. As for the pathologist, we will today commandeer all his investigations and hand over all the findings to my own people. DC Giles will be charged with obstructing justice. We will alter the autopsy result and prove Berwick Stewart's death was an accident. If I'm feeling cruel, I could make you pay for your mistakes. I could make a case against your mistress, Catherine Stewart. You need to consider that.'

Mark started to protest but Neil slapped him across one cheek. 'This is all your mistake. You went rogue and thought you could sort all this on your own. Petrou's expendable. Do you understand?'

Walking to the coach station, Diana hesitated at the post box, thinking about what she had written, before letting go of the envelope.

My Darling James

It's a hot afternoon, clammy too, bit unusual for the Lakes. Ambleside is crowded but I've found a corner of the Flying Fleece to hide in. We ate here, the one time we came for a break. You remember the Italian lady with the tattoos, always dressed head to toe in black? She served me again. I so regret I can't be with you on our 25th anniversary.

I have admitted my actions that horrible day and let all the press and my colleagues know. That means I can't be in the Police any longer.

I have to go away, so may not see you and the kids for a long time. I have to prevent a real injustice happening and it's better if I keep it all to myself. I can promise you I am in a much better place. The reality is, I feel God has forgiven me but I will have to live with however the families and others feel about me now. I have recommitted my faith and I have a chance to do the right thing.

You will be approached by MI5 and the Police demanding that you tell them where I have gone, so you can show them this letter. I suggest you go and stay with those relatives in Spain to escape the authorities and the press. I love you so much.

Diana xx

St George's church wreaked of decay and apathy. An anonymous location to meet an anonymous man. Nobody noticed Wiley, the average height, average build, M&S dressed black man, expressionless. A master of his deceitful trade, forgery. Diana first nicked him in ninety-eight, ever since, trading favours for information.

Wiley handed over a passport and a driving licence. 'Diana, why Greek, why Elena Kazan?'

Diana shrugged, tapped her nose with her finger, mouthing her thanks. The passport was perfect. Pictured with short dark hair.

Part Three

Forgiveness

*In him we have redemption through his blood, the
forgiveness of sins, in accordance with the
richness of God's Grace.*
Ephesians 1:7

36

Shelter from the storm

August 17th

After a two-hour coach ride, Diana arrived at Newcastle's ferry port for the overnight journey. She found a quiet corner to sleep before Amsterdam. Waking at six, she ate a full English fry up, without the hated mushrooms, and went ambling on the deck. The North Sea was calm for once under a blue, sunshine sky. She lent on the railings and replayed her last conversation with Neil Denver and that word he used to justify his actions. What was it? Consequentialism. She had to look it up and remembered the definition. The judgement on the rightness or wrongness of one's conduct and its moral worth is determined by its potential consequence, not by edicts or laws. She couldn't think of a single thing more at odds with her faith but since July she learnt this was how MI5, how government operated, even if innocent people died. She strolled around the deck, thinking over her next actions.

Diana went through Amsterdam passport control without a hitch and headed for the coach station. The first coach of the morning took her an hour out of Amsterdam, to the nearest town with a car rental. She hired a VW Polo with a European road map and, from a local shop, water, ham sandwiches, toffees, all paid for in cash. She brought with her the essential leather gloves. She traced a route through Germany and Switzerland away from the main crossing points and toll roads, over the Alps into Italy. Keeping to the speed limits she reckoned a twelve-hour non-stop drive.

It might be a cat and mouse game. Would they guess she swapped passports or find Wiley? She had laid some false trails. She had slipped her charged phone into the back of a pick-up heading down the M1. Hoping that MI5 were monitoring her calls, she rang James, saying she was trying to reach Spain as well. Her hair was now dyed black and Wiley remembered the specs with plain lenses.

On the outskirts of Milan Diana slept the night in the car. At a café on the E35 she was suffering the torment of Italian fried bacon, more fat than meat, but the expresso was excellent. The chat on the café television seemed to be about another Italian scandal, until her image flashed onto the screen. If only she could speak Italian. It took two more motorway services to find an internet café. The news on the BBC was that a senior policewoman was a fugitive on the run, having stolen government secrets to sell to an unnamed foreign power and may have been implicated too in the murder of an ex-soldier. The news was that DC Stephanie Giles had been arrested on suspicion of aiding her escape but was released on bail. She engaged an American backpacker in conversation who was willing to lend his phone. She texted Wiley to go see Steph and tell her what she was doing and where she was heading . Consulting the map, it was a four-hour drive away, a minor detour to fulfil an obligation.

August 18th

Siena was a wondrous step back in time, the embodiment of a medieval city. She parked the car on the outskirts and headed towards the Piazza del Campo. The Piazza was crowded with flitting tourists. She settled into a café admiring the Torre Del Mangla casting its thin, dark shadow in the sunshine. She used the café phone to call the remembered number. She closed her eyes and pictured the paraded pageantry of the famous Palio. The gathering hysteria of thousands squeezed into the Piazza del Campo, swathed in Tuscan dust, screaming as eight horses charged chaotically around. Then imagining, after the race, the Palio crowd strolling to the exits, kicking away the detritus, and the lingering aroma of animal sweat.

She raised her baseball cap to sweep away the sweat through her hair, then heard the irritating squeak of rubber soled shoes on the cobbles. A young waiter in stained black trousers, open necked white shirt, and a three-buttoned waistcoat, approached her table.

'Buona giornata signora. Cosa posso prenderti?'

'Caffè nero per favore.'

It was twenty minutes later when she saw her walking towards the table. Amina was beautiful. In her thirties she guessed. Straight, wavy, black tresses over one side of her tanned face with a gentle smile. Diana waved.

She sat down. There was no preliminary chat. 'How did my brother die?'

Diana tried to break the news kindly. Amina burst into desolate tears attracting the attention of all the other customers. Diana offered a hand to hold but she lowered her head against her chest and Diana reached over and held her arms. They stayed like this until Diana let go. 'I regret I can't do more.'

Amina wiped the tears from her cheeks. 'How did you know him? You ex-Army? You were in Bosnia?'

'No, I am no more than an acquaintance and spent time with him during his visit to Cumbria. He seemed to be a decent person. I was coming to Italy and thought you should hear what happened.'

Diana related the tragedy of three men and Vokovic walking on Morecambe Sands. One of the team pulled up hurt and her brother walked on alone, getting caught and dying in quicksand. Amina sat in silence, listening, slumped, as Diana explained how much he loved her and her children.

Diana hid the actual events. For Amina's own safety she shouldn't be contacting the Police. An hour later, after her

212

reminiscences about the faithful, tenacious, loving brother, Diana felt regretful to leave, for the fanciful story woven and the irony of again hiding the truth.

The five-hour straight drive to Brindisi brought the last challenge. Searching the docks, Diana found a freight steamer headed for Santorini and a Captain willing to take cash for the journey. Diana retained her fluency in Greek, therefore the concoction of being a hotel worker hurrying to get back home was believed. Her windowless cabin was in the bowels of the steamer. Diana slept at last. She used the Captain's phone to call her cousin, getting Tasos to find a house where she could hide out and to meet her at the harbour.

August 19th
Ships horns woke her as they sailed into Rhodes harbour. Her presence in the galley was acknowledged by a few nods. Breakfast was delightfully Greek with Epirot pie, cheese, yogurt with honey and flat bread, all washed down with stewed coffee and orange juice. Sweet mouthfuls of refreshment. On deck the Captain pointed to some chairs near the bow. Diana stretched out her legs and thought, real sunshine, real heat, nothing but the beautiful azure blue Mediterranean to silence her thoughts and rest her body after the hectic last two days. She stayed in the one spot the whole eight hours to Santorini, feeling at last like she was going home. But where was home? She was a kid in Santorini and the City was all about being a policewoman. To her surprise the Lakes began to inflict their magic on her, beautiful, captivating, magnetic as she thought back to all those mornings on her balcony with the view of the fells and Windermere. She remembered when she climbed up, towards a summit and had felt the imposing, domineering impact of the beguiling scenery and what made the place exceptional. Climbing you escaped from the world below. The effort needed drove all other thoughts away. Choosing each step carefully,

sensing the achievement and possible danger. Was there ever a locale where you could go from brilliant sunshine to being engulfed in cloud in a few hours? Where visible paths dissolved away. A welcome escape for a different life perhaps. She lost the train of thought as the boat bounced on a wave. Diana checked her backpack was still by her side. One flash stick was hidden inside her jacket, the other was sown into the strap.

That one inclusion at the end of Denver's report, to his superiors, was unfortunate. The encrypted message to the Head of Station laid out the bare facts on the incident on Blencathra and that French and Manners were both back in line. But the mistake was saying that Stewart's files were in his possession and both Petrou and Giles were dealt with. He was yet to find that was untrue and had boasted the project was now back on track. An hour after he sent the report, his phone rang. It was one of the chief scientists at GCHQ, Peter Diamond.

'Pardon, say that again Peter.'

'I'll say it again. Stewart's formulae are incomplete in the documents you sent us; a significant part was removed.'

'What does that mean?'

The scientist launched into detailed mathematics, before Denver screamed, 'STOP.'

Silence reigned.

'Forget all that. Tell me you can fix this.'

'Neil, you don't get this at all do you. Berwick Stewart was an expert in his field. He made a breakthrough that others tried and failed at, to the point where it was thought impossible. He slaved away on this for years, painstaking work. If you think I can pick it up and solve it, you're a fool. It'll take me years and that's with support from others. Get it?'

'Well you better get started.'

'Stewart was brilliant. I suggest you start looking for the missing part, otherwise all our plans will go up in smoke. I sent people to search his office and home again. He's either hidden it where we can't find it or passed it to someone else.'

Neil slammed down the phone, hurling expletives at a blank wall. He poured himself a coffee and went over to his white board, talking to himself, drawing as he spoke. 'OK, Stewart had kept back bits of the formulae, for his own leverage. French's first mistake, killing him before we could question him. First question, where is the missing formulae. We thoroughly searched his office and home, if it were there, we would have found it.'

At that moment DC Martins walked in. 'I've got news.'

'Sit down, I'll get to you in a minute. Second question, who did he give the missing formulae to? Options, his wife. Who else? DCI Petrou, did he know her? Did Vokovic take it from him before he died? Maybe it disappeared with him into Morecambe Sands? What do you want Martins?'

'DCI Petrou has gone missing. She was due to give a statement about what happened on Blencathra but hasn't been seen for two days and her flat is empty and no answer on her mobile.'

'Martins, she may be in danger, put out an APB, that's a priority. Also, can you arrange two interviews for me? First DC Giles, see if she has any idea on where DCI Petrou is. Than Catherine Stewart. Bring them here to Ambleside.'

Neil's team were an invading army of earnest young men with banks of latest laptops, flat screens. Neil initiated a familiar missing person protocol. Checks on airports, ports, visits home, phone, and social media searches. A full day's investigation produced nothing. Neil pulled in the whole team.

'I am not giving up on other searches for Stewart's missing formulae. As she has disappeared, Petrou is our main target.'

He stood up and pointed at his team.

'There's only one explanation I can think of as to why she has done this complete disappearing act; she has the formulae. It could be on a disk, a flash stick, small enough to carry with her. From what happened with French on Blencathra, she knows what Stewart was trying to do. She may have got it in her head to finish his plan. That cannot happen, let's show some ingenuity.'

The suggestions cascaded. Checking her bank account for significant cash withdrawals to avoid using a card. Tracking her mobile, which she must have disposed of. If found it might have useful content. Lean on Giles, Stewart's wife, her family.

One of the team spoke up. 'She may have headed faraway, like the North of Scotland. If I were her, I might head abroad where I am a nobody and can't be recognised. That requires another passport. She's been a copper for thirty years, will have arrested and know fraudsters. We should see who we can track down.'

Another voice piped up. 'Why don't we manipulate the truth to our advantage. We've put out a press release that she has stolen state secrets, is being hunted for questioning about a murder and an attempted murder. Let's make sure all the facts about the bombing are released and the CCTV we have and spin a story that she has had a breakdown and threatened to kill her superior. Get it out on TV too, on the net and into the European media.

37

The end of the affair

August 22nd

Early morning, before sunrise, Wiley mustered ten associates who all owed him favours, at Carnforth service station on the M6. Each carried ten addresses in different regions of the UK and ten packets of printed documents with a letter, explaining the contents and the plans of MI5 and the government. Strict instructions were given to hand over the documents directly to each addressee only. No-one else. They all headed out at the same time. If a third made their target, it would be enough.

The list of recipients included prominent nuclear physicists, other scientists, environmental organisations, favourable politicians, specialist periodicals and science journalists of national newspapers.

'I've come from a meeting at the cabinet office. The good news or the bad news first? Coffee?'

Neil Denver shook his head. Anne Manners poured her coffee and sat at the head of the table. Neil peered over the top of his clenched hands. 'Any good news?'

Anne smirked. 'No. We both lose our jobs. Find the missing formulae before it goes public, we might get to resign with a pension. If it's made public, we are the scapegoats, simple as that. OK, where are we? The good news is that this has priority over all else and all resources are available.'

Neil slid a file of papers across the desk. 'DCI Petrou has gone on the run and is our prime suspect. She will have acquired papers and passport with another identity. We have traced down three forgers she arrested in the past and one of them, nicknamed Wiley, we are told was an informant. We have a team searching Petrou's home, leaning on any relatives and informants. In her house, we did find pictures of some of her family that are all in Santorini. She lived in Santorini until her teens and her father was a local. We have sent people to watch them and any others we can identify.'

'Why get a passport, why not hide in the UK?'

'Too much CCTV. We have people on all her colleagues and criminal associates. Going abroad is safer for her. Giles is under surveillance by us. We are intercepting any communications with her. Her husband and kids have gone off to family in Spain. My guess is she wouldn't put her family at risk by going there.'

Anne asked, 'Is Santorini all guess work?'

Neil stood, walked slowly over to Anne, grabbed both her wrists, pulling her out of her seat. 'Don't question me. Remember I have all the dirt on you. About you and French, all tasty stuff for the Sundays. I know what I'm doing. We will catch up with her and when we do, we will get back the formulae. She will meet an unfortunate accident. I will still have my job, and that's the only way you might keep yours.'

With that he dropped her back in the chair, adjusted his jacket, and left.

Breakthroughs didn't usually come this quick. Neil allowed himself a modest holler when he put the phone down. Two of the fraudsters were interviewed, with decent alibis but the third, Wiley was missing for several days. He wasn't at home, not on his phone, and several colleagues confirmed he was Petrou's informant for years and he was more than a snitch. They had developed a real friendship.

Neil's team stared at the glass walls of photos and notes, in silence, with him pleading for any breakthrough.

'Nobody, nothing? What about this man Wiley?'

A lone voice piped up.

'No trace. We found another address he used, turned it over, found nothing. No-one will let on where he does his forgeries.'

'Petrou's family in Spain and in Santorini?'

The same voice spoke again.

'Twenty-four watch on both, no sightings.'

A voice spoke out from the back of the room. Jean Front, their resident IT genius. 'Neil, we think she has forged papers, unless she is hiding in the UK. She might try flying but she knows we can have airports well covered and there's face recognition to deal with. So the other option is sailing to the continent. I've done a hunt at three ferry ports. She could risk driving south or up to Scotland, but the nearest port is Newcastle, over to Amsterdam. The thing is few passengers travel on their own. It's usually lorry drivers and some families. I have a listing of all single passengers since the 14th. Following your Santorini theory, if she is headed home, there was only one passenger on a Greek passport, name of Elena Kazan.'

'Fine Jean. Check all the coaches, trains, and car hire around Amsterdam. Get co-operation from the Dutch security to have CCTV checked at the port and we can check at Newcastle.'

Jean interrupted. 'Guv, if I were her, I'd drive south. Trains and planes have too many people to identify her with the story we have put out.'

'Ok, check the car hire companies around Amsterdam. Get on to it.'

Two hours later, Jean swept into Neil's office. 'Got her. She hired a car in that Greek name and we have the registration so we checked all the country border controls. She crossed into Italy four day ago. After that we lost her for part of a day but picked her up again on the motorway tolls going south and I would guess she is heading for Brindisi. It's a reasonable supposition she's heading for her old home Santorini, where she can get family help.'

Neil thought for a moment. 'That's still supposition. We need to get our people to Brindisi and show her photo around the port and make it clear she is a wanted person for treason. I'm going to fly to Santorini and see what we can find out from her family.'

38

Held down.

August 23rd

Early evening, Diana was staring at Steph attempting to eat multiple fries at one time, licking off her greasy fingers one by one.

'What?' She asked.

Diana shook her head, 'Nothing. You took a real risk for both of us coming here.'

'They don't know you're here. I'm just on holiday.'

'Why weren't you arrested?'

'I was but they couldn't charge me without opening up on French and Vokovic. I think they were happy I was disappearing for a while. Maybe I'll face something when I get back. I still think it's crazy. You don't have to be part of this and ruin your career.' Steph held up a chip. 'We are partners remember.'

Diana wanted to say thank you again for saving her life, for being so brave and sorry for dragging her into this mess and putting her life in danger, but she smiled and said 'OK.'

Diana's cousin Tasos smiled, putting more Retsina on the table. A local guitarist was attempting to play 'Shallow'. The order of swordfish, feta salad and fries came as individual courses, in random order with indeterminate time intervals. Diana asked, 'When will the rest of the order arrive?' the answer was always 'Endaxi'. The stray cats emerged round their feet, looking for scraps. Just another species co-existing in this idyllic place.

Tasos gave them his best table, overlooking Thira harbour a few hundred feet below. People were walking up the new zig zag path carved into the rock face. Across Santorini's bay, past the volcano, the sun was taking a last bow below a crimson horizon. Diana felt older than her forty-eight years, every ache and pain matching the lines on her face. There was a loneliness creeping in. She thought she could be seduced into thinking that living here would be the answer, with James and the boys. An uncomplicated, peaceful life. Never seeing again the worst of humanity's degradation and avarice. Never seeing again a mutilated body or dealing with people bereft of compassion or kindness. But she knew it was a delusion brought on by the beguiling nature of Santorini.

Steph spoke. 'You look miles away.'

'I was just thinking, how different the air is here. On the Fells there was a cleanliness, a freshness, which stirred you up.'

'And what's the air like here?'

'Well it's permanently warm, sort of wraps you in a blanket, the opposite of stirring you up. And it smells so different. You can always smell oregano growing wild.'

'So which do you prefer?'

'I don't know. Can you hear that now? That constant clicking, that's the drone of hundreds of Cicada.'

In the late evening, the worse for wear on the Retsina, Steph and Diana didn't notice the two men standing behind them and then the feel of guns pressed into their backs. A voice whispered.

'Come with us and don't try anything.'

In a barren four metre square, white walled, wooden-floored, swelteringly hot room under a single high skylight, Diana and Steph were sat handcuffed to wicker chairs. As a door opened behind, they strained to peer round, recognising the smooth voice.

'Seems it's déjà vu Diana. You can't escape this time.'

Neil Denver placed a chair a few feet in front of her. 'Took a few days but found you both quicker than we thought. Some investigating told us about your family history here and Giles, you coming here was a coincidence we had to follow up. DCI how did you get here?

Diana stared, grim faced, silent.

'No matter. Let's get straight to the point. You either answer our questions or we go on to some more persuasive methods. Where is the missing formulae and did you make any copies?'

Diana shrugged her shoulders.

'Let's be more persuasive then.'

A gauze bag was pulled over her face and her head pulled backwards before the water was poured onto her mouth. She tried to swallow, but it was too much, she gagged, struggling to breathe. Neil whipped off the bag. 'Again, where is the formulae?'

It took some moments before Diana recovered enough to talk.

'I'm not telling you. You kill me, you'll have nothing.'

Neil leaned back in his chair and called out, 'It appears Plan A is not working, let's go straight to Plan B. I have been sanctioned to adopt any action possible to retrieve the missing formulae. It's that crucial to the country and a few lives lost are worth the cost. So this option is your choice, not mine.'

Steph's chair was dragged around till she sat facing Diana. Neil raised his Beretta and pointed it at the back of Steph's head. 'You talk or I will kill your partner.'

Diana and Steph were taken at gun point down Thira's alleyways till their path was barred by a fire show group of six performers. The tall, bronzed men in swimming trunks, the statuesque women in one-piece swimsuits, the crowding audience a perilous few feet away. The smell of petrol pervaded the atmosphere from wooden sticks with gauze endings being set alight, twirled around their semi-naked bodies, over the heads, leaving spectacular iridescent yellow light trails that seem to make time stand still and drew gasps from the audience, with flashes from their smartphones.

Fire was juggled, tossed between the acrobats, and swallowed. The group stood back and one woman stepped forward on her own, holding a long rope. The fuel was lit. She began to swing it over her head, faster and faster as the fire spread down the rope before reaching her hand to a chorus of approval from several bystanders. Diana sensed this was their chance. He wouldn't shoot into a crowd. Neil pressed the automatic straight into her back, holding one arm tight. 'Don't get any ideas. We'll go another way,' thrusting her down a side street. Ten minutes later they reached a car park on the outskirts of the town, surrounded by cypress trees.

Neil asked. 'OK, where is it?'

Diana replied. 'It's in my cousin's car that he lets me use. The keys are in my pocket.'

Neil took the remote and a car's lights flashed a few feet away. 'Where's the flash stick?'

'Open the passenger door, it's behind the door panel.'

The man with Neil tore away at the pane and a flash stick fell on the ground. Neil bent over, picked it up and shook it at Steph and Diana. 'Are there any copies?'

He was greeted with silence. 'No matter, you aren't going to be around to tell anyone. If you'd given this up in the first place, this wouldn't be necessary. Walk on.'

The further they went from the car park, the further the streetlights faded away.

Diana could make out a figure in the shadows, walking towards them. Neil said, 'I have a surprise for you.'

Mark French strode forward. Neil whispered into Diana's ear, 'I thought he owed me for all his mistakes, letting you better him on Sharp Edge. For a recompense, he is going to dispose of my remaining roadblocks.'

Neil gripped Diana's cuffed hands and pulled her until they were nose to nose.

Diana sneered. 'Isn't this where you say, I'm doing my job, following orders. Because for all your swagger you are just another cog, and expendable like me. Finally a pathetic patriot for Queen and country rather than what's right for the world. You ever think the government will have to clean house, get rid of anyone who has learnt what has gone on in the Lakes?'

It was the first time Diana saw Neil unnerved. He pulled away before taking a moment to compose himself, straightening up into his familiar military bearing.

'You don't get it. My job? To ensure it's our truth that is seen by the public. Why bother with reasoned argument with facts and figures. That's not how power or politics operates. It's been a pleasure talking to you Diana. All you had to do was let go. Not the salvation you were imagining, I guess. I'm taking Giles with me; I have some more questions for her. We found out that she's been in contact with your snitch Wiley. She's going to tell me exactly what they've done and then she may make a useful scapegoat. But you can stay here.'

He turned to French, handing him the gun. 'Don't muck this up.'

Neil and his two henchmen walked away, dragging an unwilling Steph. French approached Diana. 'Bet you regret saving me.'

The words were spat at Diana. She was forced further forward into the darkness and then shoved down onto the grass. She rolled over and French stood astride her, the gun pointed at her chest. He squatted and placed the muzzle against Diana's forehead. French remembered the eight men lined up, on their knees, handcuffed behind their backs and Vokovic stepping forward to shoot each one in the head.

'You should have let me go on Sharp Edge. I'm not about to return the favour. You have any last words?'

'Leave my family and Giles alone. I've shared nothing with them of what I've done. You have all the material. You've won.'

French smirked. 'We haven't won. The country, your country, and my country has won. We can herald a real economic boom and be seen as the climate saviours.'

225

Diana watched French's finger wrap around the trigger. She began to pray out loud for herself, for her husband and children. French smiled. 'Touching, quaint.'

Diana closed her eyes at the sound of a fired gun.

39

Point Blank

August 23rd

The bullet was fired into the earth. French's body rocked and after an anguished scream, he fell forward, lifeless, on top of Diana. She wrestled French's body off and lay still catching her breath, adrenaline surging, until a familiar voice made her sit up.

'OK cousin?'

Tasos was standing with a baseball bat in his right hand. Diana stayed rigid, struggling for intelligible words, till he pulled her up and he hugged her shaking body.

Diana held Tasos's face in her two hands. 'How are you here? I owe you my life, thank you.'

Diana hugged him again. Tasos smiled back. 'I saw you and your friend walking out of the restaurant with three men and decided to follow.' Tasos lifted aloft the baseball bat. 'And bring this.'

'That was brave and maybe foolhardy but thank you.'

'Diana, we are family, this is what we do. I thought I'd lost you with that Fire show group but managed to trail you here. I saw the three men walk away and then this man with a gun. He never heard me coming from behind.'

Tears started to roll over Diana's cheeks, staring at her cousin. 'It's all for nothing. The tall man has got what I was hiding and he's got my colleague and will make her tell the rest of our plan.'

'Diana, I don't know what this is all about, just that it's worth killing for. Who are these people?'

'They work for the British secret service, that's all I can say. I don't want you involved in this.'

Tasos leant over French and tested his pulse. 'He's still alive just knocked out. As for me not being involved, I think that ship has sailed.'

Diana rifled through French's pockets, took his wallet, keys, and his gun, to throw away. 'What do we do with him?'

Tasos answered. 'Leave him where he is. I'm guessing it's no point him talking to the Police after he was going to kill you. But we should get away from here.'

They walked quickly back through Thira's alleyways to the restaurant. Behind the bar, Tasos poured out two large brandies and handed one over. 'Diana, these men with your friend, can't be off the Island yet. They don't have to be in a hurry, thinking you are dead. They're just waiting for that man to turn up. Doesn't strike me they would be travelling by boat, so they will be at the airport either waiting for a scheduled flight or they have a private plane to use. You forget we are a close community here; the Police are all friends and some are family. I'll make a call to get them stopped.'

Epilogue

Steph interrupted Diana's train of thought.

'What happened at the airport? How come they let me go?'

'All down to Tasos. He used his connections to get the Police to stop Denver. He made it clear that either they let you go or they would be arrested. Did you tell them anything?'

'No, I think that was going to happen on their private plane. So hopefully Wiley's job is done and the papers are out. You never told me about Wiley. How did a Kenyan get that name?'

'Ahh, I apologise about that. Wiley is a name he gave himself, after the Roadrunner cartoon, Wiley Coyote. I can't remember his real name; I think he got fed up with people pronouncing and spelling it wrong.'

'How are you? You OK about giving up being a Policewoman?'

'I'm OK. I just want to see James and my kids, but that might not be possible for quite a while. About the bombing, I'm glad the truth is out. This case was like a woollen jumper. All those lies are like stray ends you pull on but ironically tug by tug the whole jumper eventually unravels. French was evil and in the end he was brought down by his own lies.'

'But what about The Scorpion he was evil and heartless too. If you can kill without caring, without remorse just to serve your own ends, not seeing any worth in the people you kill, that's real evil.'

'Vokovic was aptly called The Scorpion. But that's what he became. He was a Bosnian and witnessed the slaughter of Bosnians by the Serbs and heard that his whole family had been massacred.'

'That's a reason not an excuse. You can still have a heart after that.'

'Who knows how any of us would be after something like that. His heart was like a ruby in a bowl of ashes.'

'Very poetic.'

'Stole it from a song.'

Diana pushed her plate to one side and turned to face the reddening sunset. 'I think if I'm ever allowed back in the UK, I'm going to settle in the Lakes. I like the way the clouds are always coming in, the paths disappearing and sheep wandering looking lost. When you're walking the stones shift under your feet, streams constantly search for new paths off the fells, and there's the perpetual waterfalls. It all overpowers you.

'Di, what do you know, the Lakes have worked their magic on you. I just hope your family will like it too.'

'I was thinking about Sharp Edge. It's a bit like being a Christian.'

'How's that?'

'Sharp edge is a narrow, rocky path you walk, and if you lose the path you will slip off down the slope. Sometimes you might be able to scramble back up, other times you might roll all the way, unable to stop yourself.'

'Have you fallen off?'

'I fell off after the bombing. The lies were unravelling me. Letting people believe that I was a hero.'

Steph smiled. 'But you've scrambled back up?'

'I have but not in my own strength. I know God has been with me through this.'

Steph said, 'You do seem very different. Like a burden's been lifted from you.'

'Does that make you think about God and faith?

There was a pause before Steph replied. 'I did find myself praying when I thought Denver was going to kill me.'

'What did you pray?'

'Please God don't let me die.' Steph paused for a moment as she remembered how she felt.

Diana said. 'So, it's not just my prayers he's answered is it?'

Steph smiled at Diana. 'No, you're right.' Steph stood up. 'Changing the subject, what's the chances Berwick's work will get out?'

'In the UK, I'm thinking it's possible. The cynic or the pessimist in me, thinks they will find a way to stop it. One of the scientists or one of the journalists might contact the government or MI5 about what they've received. They will do everything to find all the people who have been given the research. They can use threats, intimidation, D notices. They will go to all lengths to shut it all down. And they will have some narrative that it's all some fanciful conspiracy. But this isn't over yet; we can't rely on people in the UK.

'What's the plan?'

'With this copy you brought; I reckon Geneva is the first target to reach.'

'Why there?'

'First bet is the UN but that still risks the British or Chinese interfering. Another thought is the scientists nearby at CERN maybe, who will be able to understand Berwick's work.'

'If that doesn't work?'

'Maybe it's some sympathetic journalists in France or Germany. Or maybe the EU in Brussels. After Brexit the UK Government doing this would really rankle. This whole case has been about finding the truth. But to French, MI5, the Government, truth is like a warm breath on a cold morning. Gone as soon as it's breathed.

Steph sighed, 'Let's sort a plan to get off this island and find out a less obvious way travel to Geneva. Let's set off tomorrow.'

'I'd love to have a couple of more days to watch the Santorini sunset and drink some more Retsina. But you're right, this isn't finished. We need to get to Geneva.'

Appendix

Undoubtedly the Climate Crisis is the greatest threat facing the Planet. My piece of fiction dreams up a fanciful solution to one fundamental element of the crisis, providing for the energy needs of a population predicted to grow to ten billion by 2030. A variety of new nuclear energy plants are being planned but the problem of toxic waste disposal still remains.

The UN report of 2021 lays out clearly the disastrous situation we are in if no dramatic action is taken to reduce the use of fossil fuels for our energy requirements and emissions into the atmosphere. We have reached a turning point. There are still powerful voices claiming that human activity is not causing climate change and COP26 did not promise the necessary actions.

Unfortunately we may think there is little we can do as individuals and we don't want to make the sacrifices needed but it is heartening the number of young people who are prepared to lobby and to protest. If you want to be part of the advocating for action there are organisations to join such as Greenpeace, WWF, Friends of the Earth, and Extinction Rebellion. There are many books to read on the subject but at this moment I recommend reading the 2021 UN Report which details all the latest scientific evidence and the dreadful consequences of our inaction. It can be found at this web address.
https://www.un.org/en/climatechange/reports

Printed in Great Britain
by Amazon